FIRESIL

Daniel Owen is the foremost ~~~~~~~~~~~~~~~~~~~~~~~~~~~~
century. He was born in 1836 i~~~~~~~~~~~~~~~~~~~ The following
spring, his father and two of his brothers were drowned in a mining
accident that left the family 'in poverty if not in destitution'.
Although he received a little education in the town's British School,
he received his true early education in the Calvinistic Methodist
chapel to which his widowed mother belonged. When he was
twelve he was apprenticed to one of the chapel's deacons, a wise
cultured tailor called John Angell Jones. The camaraderie in that
tailor-shop, Angell Jones's prompting, and the encouragement of
his minister, the Reverend Roger Edwards, turned the boy into a
youth who loved literature. In his twenties, now a fully-fledged
tailor, he published character-sketches of local characters, and
translated an American novel. Also, like hundreds of his talented
contemporaries, he started to preach.

In 1867, he enrolled at Bala College, an academy established by
Dr Lewis Edwards mainly for the education of men who wished to
enter the ministry. His fellow-students thought highly of him as an
observant, sagacious young man, as, no doubt, did the Principal. But
after eighteen months Daniel Owen returned to Mold—ostensibly
to look after his mother and sister. I think he left college because the
vital part of him could not abide the pieties of Nonconformity or its
ministerial demands. He returned also to Angell Jones's tailor-shop.
He continued to preach on Sundays, he read avidly, and he regularly
wrote and published portraits and stories and some poems. In time
he established his own tailor-shop.

Then, when he was forty, he ruptured a blood-vessel in one of
his lungs, and from then on he was never in the best of health. But
ill as he often was, the life of his imagination flourished brilliantly.
Some of his sermons and stories about Methodist-chapel affairs
were published in *Offrymau Neillduaeth; Sef Cymeriadau Beiblaidd*

a Methodistaidd (1879), after which Roger Edwards persuaded him to write a novel. *Y Dreflan* (1881) and *Rhys Lewis* (1885) were first published in monthly parts in Edwards's *Y Drysorfa*. *Rhys Lewis*, perhaps the best of his novels, an autobiographical account of the life of a minister, mirrors Daniel Owen's own life and times, and is a masterly analysis of the complexity of fervour, faith and faddishness that was Welsh religious society in the second half of the nineteenth century. Other novels followed, *Enoc Huws* (1891) and *Gwen Tomos* (1894). In 1888 he published a collection of essays, portraits and poems, *Y Siswrn*. And, in the year of his death, 1895, *Straeon y Pentan*, here in this publication translated as *Fireside Tales*.

All these books at once revere and criticise the mind and the mores of Victorian, religious, Welsh life. Of them all, *Fireside Tales* is Daniel Owen's seemingly simplest work, in that it depicts and describes men and women in such a way as to draw homely apologues from their characters and brief histories. But, as you read these stories, I trust that you will appreciate that they are the work of the same genius of wit and wisdom—and deep humanity—that gave Wales its first great body of novel-literature.

DEREC LLWYD MORGAN

FIRESIDE TALES

By

DANIEL OWEN

Translated by Adam Pearce

Edited by Derec Llwyd Morgan

www.ylolfa.com

www.browncowpublishing.com

WELSH CLASSICS FOR ENGLISH-SPEAKING READERS
—
DANIEL OWEN SIGNATURE SERIES

First published in partnership between
Brown Cow and Y Lolfa, 2011

www.ylolfa.com   www.browncowpublishing.com

This paperback edition 2011
1

A catalogue record for this book
is available from the British Library

ISBN: 978-0-9567031-1-8

Nid i'r doeth a'r deallus yr ysgrifennais,
ond i'r dyn cyffredin

Not for the wise and learned have I written,
but for the common people.

DANIEL OWEN

*As inscribed on the
plinth of the Daniel Owen
memorial statue in Mold*

ACKNOWLEDGMENTS

The Publishers would like to thank the following for their contribution to the production of this book:

Eirian Conlon, from Bangor University (Tŷ Pendref, Mold), for pointing the publisher towards Daniel Owen's literature.

Adam Pearce, from Bangor University, for his enthusiasm, hard-work and dedication to the translation process.

Les Barker for his input on the first drafts.

Derec Llwyd Morgan for his willingness to throw in his lot on the project and to edit the book, checking it for accuracy against the original Welsh version and for contributing a brief biographical note on Daniel Owen.

Huw Powell Davies, from Bethesda Chapel, Mold, and many others who helped to fill in the background detail to the text.

And finally, The Welsh Books Council, for their help in getting this work out into the public domain.

Diolch i chi i gyd.

CONTENTS

FOREWORD TO THE TRANSLATION

The stories and character portraits contained in this volume were mostly written in 1894 and 1895, the last years of their author's life. They were not all originally conceived as a collection but comprise a mixture of existing stories and new ones penned specifically for this collection. Uncle Edward was imposed upon the older stories as a framing device for the whole.

Daniel Owen often made the claim that the stories he wrote were true, even those that were certainly fiction. Some of the stories in *Fireside Tales* however have more truth in them than most. He is recorded to have taken notebooks into the pubs, shops and other public places of nineteenth-century Mold in order to record the urban legends and old wives' tales of the day, some of which almost certainly appear here. Although Owen's novels are usually set in nameless 'towns', as are some of these stories, many of the places in *Fireside Tales* are real places. Other locations appear to be fictitious. Many of the preachers and theologians who appear in these stories can be traced to real historical people; others, given Owen's penchant for basing his fiction on people and events within his own experience, are almost certainly either real people that Owen knew, or at least based on them.

Fireside Tales, or *Straeon y Pentan* as Owen named the original Welsh volume, appears here in English for the first time. The intention has been to translate artistically but keeping to Owen's form so as to retain all of the content of the original text. Personal names have been left spelled exactly as they appear in the original; place names have been Anglicised where the English form is well-known (e.g. Mold), otherwise left in Welsh. Footnotes have been added to offer translations of names of farms, houses and other places where deemed useful to the reader, as well as to explain points of information that Owen took for granted in his nineteenth century Nonconformist audience.

Readers may perhaps feel that some of these stories lack plot or structure, a flaw Owen himself acknowledged; these readers should view this volume in the knowledge that Owen had little formal education and was treading a path that no writer in the Welsh language had trodden before. Regardless, this volume has been presented in full as it was conceived by Daniel Owen, without presuming to decide for the reader which parts may or may not be of interest.

ADAM PEARCE
Bangor, June 2011

DANIEL OWEN'S FOREWORD

TO THE READER

Several of these stories have already appeared in various magazines, and the others appear now for the first time, As I have published several novels, perhaps I should state that these are true stories. I put my tales in my Uncle Edward's mouth so as to lighten the style and make them readable for everyone. I know well that the story about Twm Cynah is told about Bendigo, Tom Spring and others. For all I know Twm Cynah has as much right to it as anyone else. I believe this book will get the reception it deserves—whatever that is. There aren't many books like *Fireside Tales* in Welsh; at least, I know of but a few, and if its appearance will encourage others to make a better collection of perfectly true stories one good aim will have been reached. Perhaps a few solid brethren will scowl as they look over these pages, and whisper—'*dotard*'; for all that, I trust that each one of the stories has its point, and that there is nothing in any one of them to lower the reader's moral tone.

DANIEL OWEN
Mold, 20 May 1895

DOLI OF HAFOD LOM

Well, said my Uncle Edward, you're now old enough for me to
tell you about some things I wouldn't have thought of telling you
three or four years ago. I understand that you're starting to walk
the path that I too walked, and that nearly every member of the
human race has walked, except for the occasional bachelor who
was born a bachelor. It seems—and my Uncle looked at me with
narrowed eyes, and I blushed to my scalp—that you believe in
your heart that there's never been anyone to compare with Mary
Jones, Y Pant, and that it will be impossible for you ever to love
anyone else. Who but Mary, you say, could make you lose sleep
and put you off your food? Who but she would cause you to be
prepared to sacrifice everything for her sake, and cause you to wish
for this thing and that, and, indeed, make you think you could
die for her? Don't deceive yourself. Perhaps the sickness will pass
soon enough, and will come to you some time again in connection
with someone else, and then you'll think no more of Mary Jones, Y
Pant, than of Malen, my serving-maid. I'll warrant you think that
your Aunt Beti was the only sweetheart I ever had? No fear! She
was the last one, and the best, I believe.

But it was about Doli of Hafod Lom[1] that I was going to talk.
I've no idea how on earth the farm acquired the name Hafod Lom,

[1] When it comes to surnames, Wales is notoriously short-changed, hence the custom of
referring to people by their profession, or in this case, their home: '*Doli of Hafod Lom*'.
'*Hafod*' is the Welsh name for an upland farmstead such as used to be occupied by migratory
herders and their livestock during the summer (with its counterpart, the '*Hendre*', occupied
during the colder months). '*Llwm*' or the feminine '*Llom*' means poverty-stricken, bare
or bleak, so '*Hafod Lom*' roughly translates as '*bleak upland farmstead*'. There are many
characters in this book who are referred to by the names of their homes.

because it wasn't as bleak as most of the farms in the neighbourhood. The house was on raised ground, and faced the morning sun, and there was a large garden in front of it. Behind the house was a big farmyard, with the stables and outhouses on one side if it. At one end of the farmyard was a big deep lake, with clean clear water flowing constantly in at one end, and a floodgate at the other where the water could be released, or stored, as needed. It was obvious from the sturdy dam that surrounded it that someone in olden times had gone to considerable effort to build the lake, and it was a great asset to the house, for one of the biggest advantages of a farm, where so many live, is plenty of pure water. The rickyard was behind the stables, and beyond that there was a grove of trees. One could go to the house in two ways, along the path that went from the turnpike to the door, or along a path that went through the grove, and past the far side of the lake and over the floodgate. Rarely did anyone walk this path at night, because of the danger of falling into the lake, and the water was very deep, as I have said, on that side of it. The house was large and old-fashioned, and the rooms extensive, and far more comfortable than usual in those days. Well, you now have a pretty good idea of the kind of place Hafod Lom was.

Now, a word or two, as the preachers say, about the tenant, Richard Hughes, as I remember him when I was a youth. Richard was a tall lean man, always wearing a grey jacket and waistcoat, and breeches and gaiters of light cashmere. Richard was thin from head to toe. His legs were lean, and because they weren't particularly straight, and because his breeches and gaiters were close-fitting, there was a lot of light between them, which made one think, looking at them, that it wouldn't be an easy task for their owner to catch a piglet or a young animal in a gap. Every aspect of his face was lean—his nose was lean, his chin was long and lean, and because he'd lost his teeth, and shaved his face clean except for an inch or so by the top of his ears, his mouth was pretty concave, and his chin and his nose were becoming closer neighbours every year.

But there was one wide thing that belonged to Richard, namely his hat, which always had a low crown and a wide brim, that looked far too big for him, and weighed so heavily on his ears that it turned a hem on them. It was said of Richard that he was very wealthy. I don't wish to say that he was a miser, but I'm quite sure that he was fond of money, so fond that it was impossible except rarely to persuade him to part with any of it. After I've said that Richard was a Methodist elder, and that he had a little squeak in his voice, you'll have a good idea again of the tenant of Hafod Lom.

Hafod's mistress, Dinah Hughes, was a comely, cheerful and generous woman, but rarely was she given the opportunity to show her generosity except in Richard's absence. The poor well knew that, and would watch the old man going to the market or the chapel before thinking of going to Hafod Lom. The mistress of Hafod was considerably younger than her husband, and had aged better. Doli was their only offspring, and she was one of the prettiest and wisest girls to wear leather. She was tall and shapely, and had a face like a picture. For all that, she was exceptionally humble, and was very close to everyone, as they say. There was little difference between her dress and the dresses of other girls of much lower rank than she. But some said that it was her father who refused to buy her grand clothes, and perhaps there's truth in that. I once heard her mother say that when Doli had a new garment, she would have to keep it for a long time before wearing it; and then, if her father noticed it the first time she wore it, and started to complain about the extravagance, the mother would say: "What's the matter with you, Richard? Hasn't the girl had this for I-don't-know-how-long; where have you been till now without seeing it?" Then Dinah Hughes would buy another similar new garment for Doli, when she knew Richard had stopped trusting his eyes. However, whatever Doli'r Hafod wore, she'd turn the heads of most of the young men of the neighbourhood; and one or two of them, I believe, had re-worded the last two lines of a the well-known old verse, and would murmur it while ploughing and everywhere:

Mi af oddi yma i'r Hafod Lom
Er bod hi'n drom o siwrne;
O na chawn yno ganu cainc,
Ac eistedd ar fainc y simdde.

To Hafod Lom I make my way,
Although it's quite a journey;
Would there that I could sing a lay,
And sit beside the chimney.

The truth was that many of us had become besotted by Doli, and the fact that her father was wealthy, and that Doli was his only offspring, did nothing to ease our sickness. Frank Price of Hendre Fawr[2], Dafydd Edwards, the carpenter, and I were the only ones who received a hint of encouragement from Doli. The Hendre family were considered to be respectable and fairly well-off, and were zealous Church-goers; and Frank was a smart enough boy, although a bit wild and irreligious. But I soon realised that Dafydd Edwards, the carpenter, was Doli's favourite, and gave up the chase, more satisfied that Dafydd was the man, and not Frank. Dafydd was a church member, and a good religious young man, and very handsome. But the strange thing was, although Richard Hughes was an elder, his favourite was Hendre's son. He gave Frank every welcome when he came to the Hafod; but poor Dafydd didn't dare show his face there. The chapel-goers greatly criticised old Richard for welcoming an irreligious boy to seek his daughter's hand, and said that his love of money was the reason for that, and yet everyone believed, I think, that Richard Hughes the elder had the root of the matter. But all the wealth in the world couldn't draw Doli's love away from Dafydd Edwards, and for that the young girl's reputation in the neighbourhood rose ever higher. Rumour had it, and it seems to me to be quite true, that Doli was having a

---

[2]See note 1. '*Mawr*' ('*Fawr*' here) means '*Large*' or '*Great*', so '*Great Winter Farmstead*'.

hard time with her father because she loved Dafydd the carpenter and refused to have anything to do with the son of Hendre Fawr.

Anyway—and this is the story—one night old Richard had gone to chapel, and Dafydd, knowing that, had gone to meet Doli at the wicket gate in the path that ran through the grove of trees that I mentioned earlier. When she went to meet Dafydd, she would always take Twm with her, a sharp little dog, who, if he heard the slightest noise, would start to snarl, and then Dafydd and Doli could part before anyone saw them. But that evening the two were so engrossed in their conversation, or else the dog recognised the footsteps that were coming down the road, that they didn't notice that anyone was approaching until old Richard was beside them. It was a pretty dark night, but as soon as Doli realised it was her father there, she ran through the trees, and the old man said:

"Are you here again, Dafydd? How many times have I told you to stop coming after this girl? No matter what you say, one word or a hundred, you'll never have her as long as my eyes are open."

That moment both of them heard a heart-breaking scream, and both of them recognised the voice. Dafydd rushed along the path towards the lake, and the old man followed him as quickly as he could. The night was dark, as I said, but Dafydd, although he was agitated, and nearly out of his mind, thought that someone had crossed the path before he reached the lake. Dafydd was a peerless swimmer, and, like a man gone mad, jumped into the lake, and was groping about in the darkness for Doli, but to no purpose for a minute or two. The scream had reached the stables where the farmhands were feeding the animals, and in a few minutes all the manservants with their lanterns were at the lakeside, and as one of the farmhands told me afterwards, when the lanterns cast their light over the lake, the first thing he saw was Dafydd having got hold of Doli holding her head above the water, and he heard her last words: "O, Dafydd *bach*[3], I'm drowning." Doli

---

[3] '*Bach*' translates literally as '*little*'. In Wales it is used as a common term of endearment.

was taken to the shore and carried into the house. She was not dead, but because of people's ignorance of how to treat those in that condition, poor Doli died within a few minutes. As she was dying, she was surrounded by her father and mother, Dafydd the carpenter, and the son of Hendre Fawr. How Frank had come there on such an occasion no one ever knew, and I don't choose to give my opinion.

The event caused a great deal of pain and gossip in the neighbourhood. I had for a long time been a frequent visitor to Hafod Lom, and was very friendly with Doli and with her father and mother. I went there the day after the accident, and I never saw in my life such grief and heartbreak. Before I left, the old man, Richard Hughes, said to me:

"Edward, will you ask Dafydd the carpenter to come to the funeral?"

Remembering his hostility towards Dafydd it surprised me to hear him say this, and I was glad to carry the message.

Nearly the whole neighbourhood had come to bury Doli, and, as was customary at funerals in those days, there was a great deal of eating and drinking at Hafod. As I was something of a favourite at Hafod, I was one of the first ones there the day of the burial. Shortly before it was time to 'lift the body', and start towards the cemetery, I was alone in a room with Richard and Dinah Hughes, and I tried to comfort them as best as I could, but their grief, as you can imagine, was excruciating. Richard looked through the window towards the farmyard at the large crowd that had come to bury Doli, and said to me: "Isn't that Dafydd there standing by himself at the far end of the yard?"

I told him that it was.

"Ask him to come here," he said.

I went immediately and brought him in. I will never forget the scene. When Dafydd came in the old man broke down completely, and he could not say a word for a long time. Once the flow had abated, he said—and his words reverberate in my ears this very moment:

"Dafydd, Oh! Dafydd, God has struck me—has struck me so as not to damn me! Doli was yours—yes, yours, and in trying to rob you of her I lost her forever! Dafydd,"—and the old man placed his head on Dafydd's broad shoulder—"it was all my fault, and God has struck me!" and he wept profusely. "Dafydd," he added, "may I lean on your arm on the way to the cemetery?"

Dafydd said all that needed to be said by squeezing the sorrowful old man's hand, and everyone was surprised to see Richard Hughes walking in Dafydd the carpenter's arm towards the cemetery.

There was much talk and gritted-teeth conjecture amongst the neighbours after this. Whether Doli met her end accidentally or otherwise, nobody ever knew. Shortly after this the son of Hendre Fawr joined the army, and was killed in East India. Richard Hughes was never the same man again. He did not live long after this; but while he lived, he showed no sign that he loved money, and he ended his life as one of the most generous and open-handed men in the country. People said that Richard Hughes, Hafod Lom in his last will left a large sum of money to Dafydd the carpenter, but I don't know if that's true. But I do know this, that Dafydd never loved anyone else again after losing Doli—he died a bachelor, and pretty well-off, said my Uncle Edward.

2

YOU DON'T BUY A WOODCOCK
BY ITS BEAK

Don't ever take people at face value, or you'll more than likely be disappointed sometimes. There's an old Welsh saying—*Nid wrth ei big y mae prynu cyffylog* (You don't buy a woodcock by its beak[1]). I remember when I was a youngster living with my mother and father in Cefnmeiriadog, that Wil Williams, the son of the farm next to us, and I were great friends; and that because our parents were in better circumstances than some of the poor farmers around us, we thought rather a lot of ourselves. You'll hear some say that the times don't get better. Nonsense; things have improved a great deal. Then, the son of a farmer was seldom seen reading a good book, unless he'd set his mind on becoming a preacher. Our main entertainment back then, I'm sorry to report, were foolish sports like running, jumping, prison bars, fights and cock-fighting. Although none of us read a newspaper, somehow we came to hear of the fights in England and in Wales, and in history we were as familiar with Bendigo Caunt, Tipton Slasher, Tom Spring, Welsh Jim, and Twm Cynah, as boys these days are with the names of Owen Thomas, John Thomas, and other great preachers[2]. One parish-festival[3] there was to be great merriment in Denbigh, and Wil Williams and I had been saving our pennies for weeks to go there. I remember that both of us had had new clothes, a velvet coat and waistcoat, striped breeches, and also a watch with a steel chain with a seal and a shell attached to it, and

---

[1] An Englishman might say, 'don't judge a book by its cover'.

that we thought ourselves quite the gentlemen. We imagined that tears flowed not only from the eyes, but also from the teeth, of our less fortunate contemporaries. In those days a stagecoach ran through St Asaph to Denbigh and from there to Mold, and from there to Chester.

On the morning of the parish-festival, Wil Williams and I —looking quite splendid, I thought—had been waiting for some time in St Asaph for the stagecoach, and were looking at our watches every three minutes or so, to allow everyone to see that we possessed such a valuable instrument. When the coach arrived, in order to show our nobility, we took our seats on the box, alongside the driver, although we knew that we'd have to tip the driver for the privilege. There was a man on the box before us—a man of about thirty-five years of age—mean and humble in appearance. He wore a grey coat, and we could see that the coat and its owner had been acquainted with each other for many years. Boldly enough we asked the man in the grey coat to change his seat so that we could sit next to the driver, and he moved obediently, without a word of complaint. The driver was a strongly-built, bulky rascal, with a nose so red that we thought he flashed its hue on everything we passed. We knew that the driver was quite a fighter, and that's why we were so keen to sit next to him—in order to hear about his exploits, and others in the same line, and in this we weren't disappointed. Of course, first we had from him his own feats, and we were open-mouthed hearing about his victories. In those days

---

[2] Owen Thomas (1812–1891), a native of Holyhead, became famous as one of the most powerful preachers of Victorian times, a writer of splendid biographies of other great Methodist preachers, and a theologian of note. There were many John Thomases. It can be presumed that the John Thomas named here was Owen Thomas's brother (1821–1892): although brought up a Calvinistic Methodist, he joined the Congregationalists, whom he served stoutly in the pulpit and in the press. In their heyday both brothers held ministries in Liverpool.

[3] 'Parish-festival' is an approximate translation of 'gwylmabsant', the holy day associated with the patron saint of a particular parish.

there was a lot of talk about Welsh Jim amongst the lightweights, and Twm Cynah amongst the heavyweights—both from Mold, as you know. Twm was a true Welshman, although his name was Cynah.

"The truth is," said the driver, "too much is being made of Twm Cynah. I'd like to have him stand before me for two minutes or so, though I never saw the man. I'd show him that there's another Welshman in the world."

Wil and I were amazed at the driver's boldness and skill. The man in the grey coat didn't say a word from his mouth, but I thought I saw a smile slip across his face when the driver was singing his own praises, something that annoyed me quite a bit. After tiring of discussing fighters, like senseless, bad boys, we began mocking everyone we passed on the road, and we didn't spare the man in the grey coat. Indeed, we were very bold with him, but he suffered everything quietly and apathetically, a fact that made Wil and me annoy him all the more. At last, the stagecoach reached the courtyard of the Crown, Denbigh, where they changed horses and the driver also. After we had climbed down from the coach, the driver stood by our side, awaiting his tip; and playing the gentleman, I gave him a shilling, and so did Wil. Then we saw the man in the grey coat fumbling in his pockets for a long time, and eventually he handed tuppence to the driver. I saw the driver's face turn puce, and he begun to chide the man in the grey coat terribly.

"What business did a ragamuffin like you have riding on the box?" he said; "the box is a place for gentlemen, and were it not that I'd hate to hit a bag of bones like yourself, I'd give you a beating to remember."

"You would?" said the quiet man; and by now a number had gathered around us. "You would?" he said; "what if you tried?" and he threw off the grey coat.

The driver was beside himself at having a chance to give a beating to a man who'd tipped him the tuppence. But pity him!

The quiet man hit him until he was spinning, and he didn't know high from low. But he came forward again, to go through exactly the same treatment, and by now the driver was not eager to get off the floor. And the man in the grey coat said:

"If this boaster wants to know more about me, my name is Twm Cynah; I live in Maesydref, Mold." And he walked leisurely to the Crown.

By now Wil and I had taken great fright, but we did what I believe was the best thing we could have done under the circumstances— we followed him into the inn to beg his pardon, and to offer to pay for as much drink as he wanted. But Twm Cynah said, and here's the lesson:

"I don't drink, thank you, boys, but take a word of advice from me. The next time you leave home, make sure you take someone to look after you. I forgive you your misbehaviour, because I know that senselessness was the cause of it. Take care they don't shut you up in the great house nearby[4]. But perhaps you've enough sense to remember this—don't ever judge people by their appearances, and don't ever mock people in the road, especially women and innocent old people. When you were tormenting that old man before we came to the town, I was never so tempted to throw the two of you and the driver as well over the hedge, which I could have done easily. Another thing: when you hear someone sing his own praises as that driver did, consider him an idiot."

I never forgot Twm Cynah's advice, and it was a life-long lesson for me, said my Uncle Edward.

---

[4] Denbigh asylum, which opened in 1848. The facility was substantial, housing 1500 patients at its peak. Jibes such as 'you might end up in Denbigh' were used by some, less gracious locals right up until its closure in 1995.

3

THE TWO BONNERS

William and Richard Bonner were strange old fellows, said my Uncle Edward. I've a fairly good memory of the two, but not good enough to give a description of them. Both were natives of Gwernymynydd, near Mold. William was a preacher, and Richard a minister, not unrenowned, with the Wesleyans. It was recognised that Richard Bonner was an especially witty man, and his brother William was not deficient in that gift. Fifty years ago, it was a well-known fact that William Bonner and 'The Old Sole' were the two strongest men in the parish, if not in the county. 'The Old Sole' carried ten cubic feet of solid oak on his shoulders, and William Bonner carried half a ton of Maeshafn lead (and everyone knows that Maeshafn lead is heavier than other leads) in a sack on his back, and the two Samsons were judged equal in the Gwernymynydd National Eisteddfod, and the prize was shared. William Bonner, like his brother Richard, was a particularly acceptable preacher among the Wesleyan brotherhood, and indeed among everyone else. You know full well that in those days lay preachers received very little for their services, and I fear that they still don't receive as much as they deserve in our day. But some believed then, as many think now, that preaching paid excellently, and that men of the white neckcloth were making a fortune.

"How much do you get for this preaching, Wil?" said Shôn, Pant Glas[1], to William Bonner once; and William said:

"Well, I expect the crown, you know, Shôn."

"Dear me!" said Shôn, "a crown in the morning, a crown in the afternoon, a crown in the evening, that's fifteen shillings?

---

[1] *'Pant Glas'* literally translated means *'Green Hollow'*.

Who wouldn't be a preacher?"

William did not take the trouble to explain to Shôn that he meant the spiritual crown. William Bonner was one of the first to take the temperance pledge, about the year 1834 or '35, and he was very zealous as was his brother Richard. Once he was to give a lecture on temperance in Gwernymynydd, and Tomos Owen, Tŷ'r Capel, Mold, was to be his chairman. Tomos Owen was a very strange man, and I'll have a story to tell you about him some evening when I remember. He was a Methodist preacher, and the son of Richard Owen, Bala. But Tomos Owen, although he was a preacher and a very godly man, was, as people generally were in those days before the temperance movement began, rather fond of his half pint, and although Tomos was among the first to take the pledge, some believed that he took the occasional drop on the sly. William Bonner had heard the gossip about his friend, and as he began his lecture on abstinence, after the chairman, Tomos Owen, had introduced the lecturer to the meeting, he said:

"Friends, some people are spreading the story in this neighbourhood that our respectable chairman, Tomos Owen, and his wife Marged, drink beer from the spout of the teapot, but they're lying through their teeth, aren't they, Tomos?"

"Yes, indeed," said Tomos, "I never drank a drop of beer from the spout of the teapot, nor Marged either," and the two were never slandered again.

But it was about Richard Bonner that I meant to talk to you this evening, but I keep rambling. I heard him preach more than once, but I was too young to be impressed, except to note that he was a droll and witty man. I subsequently heard tens of amusing stories about him, but at the moment only two come to mind. The Wesleyans have a chapel that's called Tafarn y Celyn[2], or, as it's pronounced by country folk, Tafarn-gelyn, a place on the way from Mold to Llanarmon. At one time there was a faithful and

---

[2] '*Tafarn-y-celyn*' literally translated means '*Holly Inn*' or '*Holly Bush Inn*'.

very godly old woman called Begws who was a refined member of Tafarn-gelyn chapel. Her circumstances were poor, and the old woman received some parish relief. Through the years Begws kept a pig, and once it grew to a certain size she'd sell it to pay the rent on her cottage. But on one occasion some carcass of a man stole Begws's pig, and caused her great tribulation. The church at Tafarn-gelyn felt keen sympathy for the old woman in her loss, and, Christian-like, they decided to make a collection for her in the evening service on the Sabbath. Richard Bonner was to preach on the night of the collection, and the chapel deacons asked him to say a word about the matter, for they were eager to compensate poor old Begws, and before the collectors went around Bonner said:

"Well, friends, we all know Begws—as she's got nothing spare she'll have peace from petty thieves, and I know that everyone will give as much as he can in this collection apart from the man who took the poor creature's pig. You can be sure that the man who stole the pig won't put a halfpenny on the plate!"

Every soul contributed so as not to be suspected of being guilty of stealing Begws's pig, and the old woman received far more than she had lost.

Richard Bonner was a strong and powerful man, and you know that when a Wesleyan minister has been itinerate for a certain number of years in the ministry he has the right to put himself on the supernumerary list, that is to free himself from the cares of the circuit. Old Bonner had served faithfully for the required period, and in a district meeting he made an application to be considered a supernumerary. The brotherhood couldn't see its way clear to allow this because at the time they had nobody to take his place, or some other excuse, and the president of the province as a preface to persuading Mr Bonner to withdraw his application said:

"Well, Mr Bonner *bach*, we all know that you've the right to ask to be made a supernumerary, but, up to now, you're strong, you don't cough, and you preach well— "

The president wasn't allowed to go any further before the smart old man stood on his feet, and he said:

"Oh dear, if coughing is what's needed, I can cough as well as any of you, but if you want to wait until I preach poorly, I will never get to be made a supernumerary."

I don't remember how things ended with regards to Mr Bonner's application, but that'll do to show you the man's smartness and his ready wit. If no biography has been made of Richard Bonner, then there's an amusing and beneficial task awaiting someone.

4

THE RECEIPT

Here's one of the stories my Uncle Edward loved to tell, because they were, as he said, completely true:

You know that the Methodist cause in town is an old cause—one of the oldest in the county. In olden days people didn't contribute half as much as the religious people of today, and there wasn't as much need. Although a minister and two preachers were attached to the cause in town, in part doing pastoral work, nobody thought to give them a halfpenny for their labour. They would receive a small amount for preaching, and that's all. But however small the contributions, the folk had paid for the chapel years since, and they had money in the treasurer's keeping. The old people were rather inept at treating financial matters—everything was left to two of the elders, and everyone trusted them as honest men, and nobody ever asked to see the accounts, and if anyone did they would regard it as an insult. Indeed, their fellow elders were not privy to their confidentiality—quite phlegmatically they wholly accepted their year-end report. In those days many would come from considerable distances to the chapel in town, especially from Gwernhefin, and in their midst two brothers—two responsible farmers. In time, the two brothers made an appeal to be allowed to establish a cause in Gwernhefin, for walking the two-mile journey to town three times was tedious. The town people consented, and soon a small chapel was built there to hold Sunday School in the morning, and to hold the afternoon service led by the preacher who happened to be in the town. This is how things remained for some years until a branch church was established there, when Edward and Thomas Williams—the two brothers—were made elders at Gwernhefin. Within a few years they had paid the cost of building the small chapel, less forty pounds, and, as it was known that the folk in town had money in hand, they made a request to borrow forty pounds interest-free, and said that the money would be repaid when called for, and this was permitted. After receiving the loan, the people of Gwernhefin became unconcerned about paying their debt.

A man by the name of John Evans belonged to the church in town, a prominent man with the cause whose chief peculiarity was the tediousness of his prayers. Our knees would stiffen up every time John Evans was called upon to pray. Although elders were appointed on several occasions during John Evans's stay there, each time he was left unelected. But John Evans compensated for this by praying for as long as three every time he was given the opportunity. Eventually, the people of the town needed money, and the fellows at Gwernhefin were called upon to repay the forty pounds. After many concerts, lectures and tea parties, the money was collected. Years passed, and by now the financiers of the town chapel had died, and John Evans had moved to Gwernhefin, and had been elected an elder there. As they had done in the town, so they did in Gwernhefin—the two brothers kept every financial confidentiality to themselves, but they were men of transparent character, and of unquestionable godliness. About a year after John Evans's election as elder, Edward, one of the brothers, died, and all confidentiality fell into Thomas's bosom alone. Soon, for some reason or other, John Evans became stubborn, and refused to take any public part in the chapel. He would regularly come to the meetings to scowl. One Sunday evening, in the *seiat*[1], after earnestly urging him to speak and after he had refused, Thomas Williams said:

"John Evans, what's wrong with you? For a while now you have refused to do anything; who has offended you? Let us hear."

---

[1] The word '*seiat*' comes from the English '*society*', more especially from the term '*private society*'. It refers to a religious meeting amongst early and nineteenth-century Methodists characterised by sharing personal religious experiences, counselling, prayer, &c— a religious meeting usually held on a weeknight.

John Evans stood on his feet, and he said:

"Thomas Williams, will you answer this question—did you pay the forty pounds that Gwernhefin church borrowed from the church in town?" and he sat down, and everyone was stunned, no-one more so than Thomas Williams himself.

"Paid them?" said Thomas Williams, "yes, rather, of course, and I've got the receipt in the house. I take great care to keep every receipt."

"All right," said John Evans, "bring it here, if you can."

Every soul in the meeting, except John Evans, believed that Thomas Williams would be able to present the receipt, and having left the meeting, several of the brethren attacked John Evans for his impudence. But all he would say was: "Wait awhile to see if he can find the receipt." Thomas Williams had a large, respectable family, and the next day they all went to search for the receipt. There were many hundreds in the house—some of them fifty years old, but they failed to find the necessary receipt, and a wretchedness weighed heavily upon Thomas Williams and the family. Everything in the house was turned upside down; every nook and cranny was searched diligently, but to no avail. The old man could neither sleep nor eat, and by the next *seiat* meeting he had become emaciated.

After the initial service in the *seiat*, John Evans stood up, and he said:

"Thomas Williams, did you bring the receipt for the forty pounds with you tonight?"

"I did not," said the old elder. "The children and I have tried our best to find it, but so far we've failed to find it. But I'm certain that I paid the money, and I think that the church here believes my word. I shall go to town tomorrow to Owen Jones's daughter, and no doubt there's documentary evidence in her father's old books to show that I have paid the money. Owen Jones and my brother are in their graves, else they'd be able to testify to the truth of what I'm saying."

"I've been to town before you," said John Evans, "and there's no documentary evidence in Owen Jones's papers to show that you have paid, and no-one in the church in town remembers you paying a halfpenny of the money."

"God is my judge," said Thomas Williams, "I paid the money honestly, and I'm sure I'll be able again to show that I'm telling the truth."

Thomas Williams made detailed enquiries among the town folk, and amongst others, but nobody remembered him paying the money. By now the matter was the talk of the country, and many of the members at Gwernhefin believed as John Evans believed. But the majority firmly held to the belief that Thomas Williams was an honest man, for he was an affluent man for whom money was not a care. Thomas Williams and family had been the cause's main support for half an age, and no house in the district had been open to receive preachers except theirs, Trosygarreg[2]. Things went from bad to worse, and it's easier to imagine than to describe Thomas Williams's thoughts, and his family's. The matter was brought before the Monthly Meeting[3], and two ministers and an elder were appointed to go to Gwernhefin 'on a special matter', and it was believed by many that Thomas Williams would not only be relieved of his position as elder, but would also be stripped of his church membership.

The evening of the trial came, and as is the case in such situations not a fingernail was absent from that *seiat*. Thomas Williams seemed to be scowling and determined, and his sons held their heads high, and some people said that it would be more appropriate for them to have stayed at home or else keep their heads down. After the younger minister had read and prayed, referring in the prayer more than once to the uncomfortable occasion, and after

---

[2] '*Trosygarreg*' literally '*Over the Stone*'.

[3] The Monthly Meeting brought together the officers or representatives of individual Methodist churches in a defined area to discuss matters pertaining to their common causes.

the children had recited their verses and had been sent home, the older minister set out the matter they had come to discuss clearly and importantly before the church, and not without a great show of heartfelt grief, for he and the accused had been great friends. Then, very tenderly, he asked the veteran elder what he had to say for himself. Thomas Williams rose to his feet amid a deathly silence, and said, as accurately as I can remember, thus:

"The forty pounds were borrowed thirty-five years ago, and I paid them twenty-five years ago last Wednesday. You can easily imagine my feelings ever since John Evans made this accusation against me. The whole time I have slept and eaten only a little. From that day I and the children have searched every corner of the house for the receipt, but to no avail; and thinking about your coming here tonight, and the reason for it, was as if someone put a dagger in my heart. Today for the hundredth time the children and I searched the house from top to bottom to look for the receipt, but to no purpose. Whilst we were trying to drink a cup of tea, I told them: 'Well, children, your father will be expelled tonight, but my conscience is clear of the blame that has been placed against me', and here the old elder broke down, and we had to wait a minute for him to collect himself, and he added: "After tea I locked myself in the parlour to await the *seiat*, and if I ever prayed I certainly prayed this evening. I felt that God was dealing pretty harshly with an old servant. I must confess my weakness that I upbraided him quite a bit. I told him that I had tried to serve him since I was a boy, that I had contributed to his cause according to the way he had made me succeed in the world, that I had opened my house to welcome his servants all through the years, and I asked him if he was going to cast me aside in old age, and I'm not sure if I didn't even suggest to him that might not be honourable. Anyway, I felt better after telling him that; and I left everything to him, but did so having all but told him that I would watch how he treated me. There was yet some time before the *seiat*, and I thought I would try and read a little to pass the time. I reached for an old volume of *Y Drysorfa*[4] from the shelf, and God knows that I am telling the truth, where the book opened, there was the receipt! I shouted all over the place—receipt! receipt! receipt! and the children came to the door, thinking I had lost my senses, and that wouldn't have been strange, and I didn't remember that I had locked the door, and I was still shouting receipt! Once I had calmed down and opened the door, we went on our knees. Here's the receipt, Mr E——, and you are quite familiar with Owen Jones's handwriting," and Thomas Williams sat down, and I must say there was barely a dry eye in the place.

"W—w—well, Mr Williams," said Mr E——, "there have been many good things in *Y Drysorfa*, even if I, the Editor, say so myself, but this is the best thing you ever found in it."

I cannot describe to you, said my Uncle Edward, our feelings that evening. Everyone except for John Evans was crying tears of happiness. He looked as if he'd been shot. Yet some believed that John Evans had been quite sincere in his suspicions, even though he was mistaken. He did not live long after this, and looked like a broken-hearted man.

---

[4] *Y Drysorfa* = *The Treasury*; a Methodist journal in which many of Daniel Owen's own writings were published.

5

ENOC EVANS OF BALA

Yes, said my Uncle Edward, I remember Enoc Evans of Bala quite well. Enoc and I didn't hit it off very well—he'd come into the world a little early, and I a little late, and so not much of an acquaintance was formed between us. But I heard a lot about Enoc as one who was a peerless reader, and very fond of birds. Nobody in his right mind would arrive late at chapel when Enoc was to preach, because hearing him read the chapter was the treat. He was not, as I heard men of good judgement say, much of a preacher. In these days, Castle Street is the lowliest and dirtiest street in Mold. I don't believe that there is or that there ever was a single house there with a back door, and most of the houses have by now been deemed unfit for human occupation. But the old street has a sacred history. If Castle Street could tell its own story, it would have plenty to say, and of considerable interest. In the first house on the right lived old Angel Jones[1], the famous elder for whom Glan Alun wrote an excellent elegy. Angel raised a large family in this cabin, and did huge business as a tailor. The house has only two bedrooms, and another small one on top of the stairs, and yet, strange to think, it was the main home of some of the most famous people of the Welsh pulpit on their visits to the town. In this tiny insignificant house slept Eben and Thomas Richards, William Harvard, Roberts Amlwch, John Elias, the two Joneses of Llanllyfni, Henry Rees, and a host of others, when they came to Mold to preach, and among them Enoc Evans of Bala.

---

[1] There is little doubt that Angel Jones in this story is based on Angell Jones, Daniel Owen's early master and mentor. Most likely it was also Angell Jones who provided the inspiration for the character of Abel Huws, who appears in Owen's novels *Rhys Lewis* and *Enoc Huws*. Glan Alun was the bardic name of poet Thomas Jones (1811–1886).

At the top of Castle Street lived a strange character—you remember him well—called William Jones, a tailor all his life. He was commonly known by the name Cwil. He was a short, erect man, always wearing a dress coat and a top hat. Cwil was neither a Welshman nor an Englishman, but he had a grasp of both languages. His mental capacities were very feeble, and after growing up he spent three months trying to learn the Lord's Prayer, and in the end had to give up the endeavour as a bad job. Cwil loved two things above all others, beer and birds. He would sometimes have a long bender, and I heard him say that he'd lost three days of his life about which he knew nothing. Cwil had had a week's spree, and slept from Saturday night until Wednesday morning without waking. Every Saturday night of the year, after receiving his wages, and washing and shaving, Cwil would go for his liquor to the Talbot, and he would drink so heavily that when leaving the tavern he knew nothing except that the way home was 'to turn to the right'. But one Saturday he was persuaded by a companion to go to the Eagle and Child, on the other side of the street. As he set off home that evening Cwil remembered the rule about turning right, and on Sunday morning found himself at Pentre Hobin on the Wrexham road, lying in a ditch, and unable to figure out how he had failed to follow the usual landmarks. But as I said, Cwil was very fond of birds—even more so than of beer. Once, when Enoc Evans was preaching in Mold, old Angel happened to mention Cwil Jones's birds to him. Enoc went there immediately, and Cwil and he talked about birds till midnight, and would have continued till morning had Angel not gone to fetch his lodger.

After this, Cwil would ask Angel every day: "Hengel, when's the bird merchant coming to preach here again?" And when Enoc Evans came across country to Mold, the first thing he would do, before having a bite to eat, was to visit Cwil, and talk about the birds, and on many occasions in Cwil's company Enoc would have forgotten all about his food and the service and everything, had Angel not been at hand. Once, Enoc Evans had taken a rare fancy to a canary that was in Cwil's possession—he doted on it as a singer, and the old fellow sat down to listen to it for hours. The next time Enoc came to Mold, after putting his horse to stable in the Black Boy, he went straight to visit Cwil Jones, and after looking over the house, he said:

"Where's that splendid canary gone, William Jones?"

"The cat's killed it, Mister Hivans," said Cwil.

"Was the culprit your own cat, William?" Enoc asked.

"No fear," said Cwil, "I'd kill every cat in the world if I could."

"And I'd help you, William," said the old preacher.

"I'm glad to hear you say, Mister Hivans," said Cwil, and added with a sigh, "It was John Bowen's cat what killed it, and I wouldn't take its weight in gold for that bird, Mister Hivans. And I'll tell you what I did with it, sir—the cat, you know—I caught it on Saturday as it came into the house to look for another bird, and I put it in a box with a lock on it, and on Sunday morning I filled my pipe and took a stool into the garden, and I got the cat and hung it from the apple tree, and I sat on the stool to watch it die, and I got my revenge."

"And serves the slattern right," said Enoc zealously, and he added, "I see, William, that you've got some chicks here."

"I do, Mister Hivans," said Cwil, "but you've never seen trouble like I had getting them. I tried a hen with that cock for weeks, and the two'd have nothing to do with each other; but I tried another hen with the cock, and I got chicks soon, which proves it wasn't the fault of the cock."

"My dear, dear me!" said Enoc.

"Enoc Evans, it's time to go to the chapel," said Angel at the door; and the two old fellows' *seiat* was interrupted.

No sooner was the meeting over that Enoc strode back before Angel to Castle Street. When Angel came to the house, he found that Nancy had made supper, but that there was no sign of Enoc Evans. Angel guessed where the old preacher was, and off he went to Cwil Jones's house, and he found the two in deep discussion about the birds.

"William Jones," said Enoc, "why is it that you don't keep anything but these canaries and goldfinches? Don't you like other birds?"

"I do, Mister Hivans," said Cwil, "I like all sorts of birds. But you see that the house is a mite small, and a bird of paradise or a blackbird needs a big cage, and they're a bit dirty. But I wouldn't mind that if I had the space for them, Mister Hivans. And I tell you something else, Hangel knows as well as I do, I was specially fond of larks, and had one once I never saw its like. It was me what brought it up, and he was a singer like I never heard. And he was so tame that I took him to the workshop, as Hangel knows. Well, once I took him to the workshop, and there was a man, his name was George Roberts, he sang in church—the best bass singer you ever heard—but he had no respect for a good bird. Well, I took the bird into the shop I tell you, Mister Hivans, and after I sat on the table, I held the lark in the palm of my hand— it was ever so tame—and I said, 'There you are, George, a bird whose sort you never saw.' And what George did, without me thinking, he took a stick and struck me under my elbow, and I fainted. When I came to, I asked, 'Where's my lark, George?' And I saw the lark dead on the table. After that I'd had enough of keeping larks."

"Well, the ungodly and callous man," said Enoc. "What did you—?"

"Enoc Evans, it's high time you came to the house," said Angel.

I stayed in Bala for a while, said my Uncle Edward, and during that time I got to know two of Enoc Evans's sons. One was a stonemason, and his name was Dafydd, if I remember correctly. In those days it was a gloomy period for religion, and work was scarce. To get more work, Dafydd left religion and went to the Church[2]. But soon a religious revival visited the town of Bala, and it was a wonderful time for the fellowship in the old chapel. One

---

[2] That is, the Established Church, the Church of England.

seiat evening, when the revival was at its hottest, Dafydd came back to his old home, and Dr Lewis Edwards[3] went to discuss matters with him. The discussion, as close as I can remember, went like this:

"Well, Dafydd Evans, what made you return?" said the Doctor.

"I failed to be comfortable during this revival in that old Church," said Dafydd.

"There are very good people in the Church," said the Doctor.

"Yes," said Dafydd, "people who are very good at caring for the body, they beat you here hands down for that. I was getting far more work in the Church than when I used to come here. But they're pretty poor at caring for the soul."

"Well," said the Doctor, "I heard that Church folk care for the soul as well. During this revival the Church had prayer meetings as we had in the chapel, didn't it?"

"It did, Mr Edwards," said Dafydd, "but do you know which verse came to my mind while watching them at it?"

"No, indeed, I don't," said the Doctor.

"And the sorcerers did in like manner[4]," replied Dafydd, and the Doctor split his sides laughing.

---

[3] Dr Lewis Edwards (1809–1889), a native of Pen-llwyn, Ceredigion, was the chief scholar amongst 19th-century Methodists: he founded Bala College as an academy for prospective ministers, he helped found and edited the quarterly journal *Y Traethodydd*, in which he published splendid essays on literature and theology, and was a greatly respected preacher. He often took part in the services of the Methodist chapel in Bala.

[4] This is a quote from Exodus 7:11 which recounts Pharaoh's magicians counterfeiting the miracles performed by Moses and Aaron with more dubious 'miracles' of their own. Owen took it for granted that his audience had a reasonable knowledge of biblical matters and would understand the background story to the verse. Dafydd Evans seems to be implying that—in his own opinion—the Anglicans were merely copying the chapel's authentic revival meetings by holding less inspired gatherings of their own.

6

JAC JONES'S HAT

You've heard many times that the mind has a lot to do with the health or the sickness of the body, and that's true enough. Here's a story for you that's as true as the Lord's Prayer.

By the time I was a young man, I'd long been fed-up of working on the farm—it was too quiet a life for me. I'd heard that there was a good wage for young men in Mold's cotton mill, and I went there to find work. I was immediately employed as a kind of errand-boy for the spinners, and I was quite happy with my position. There was another youth there of about the same age as me in the same job—a boy who'd lost one eye, but who saw more with his one than boys generally saw with their two eyes. His name was William James, and he was a very mischievous lad, and we soon became good friends. William and I were accomplices in some tricks played daily on the spinners. But it was tacitly agreed between Wil and myself that we were to take it in turns to take the blame. If I were accused of the mischief, Wil James would take the blame, just as I would when he was accused. Thus, we would avoid one chastisement, and the spinners were terrible for chastising. The spinning-room foreman was Thomas Burgess, one of the cruellest and least popular men with the workers that I ever saw. But Burgess was very fond of joking and playing tricks on the men under his care, and so Wil James and I were not too low in his esteem.

I had read somewhere that it was possible to persuade a healthy man to be sick, and a sick man to be healthy, if his sickness wasn't a particularly bad one. One lunch hour I mentioned this to Thomas Burgess, and he replied:

"It's quite easy to put this to the test if you and Wil James put your heads together to experiment on one of these chaps. If Wil can't devise something in that way, there's no point in you and I trying, because Wil is a rascal of a chap." Wil felt the same about Burgess, that he too was a rascal.

"You know what," Wil told me one day, "I'd like to die the same minute as old Burgess."

"Why's that?" I said.

"Because he's got so much to answer for," said Wil, "and while they were dealing with his case, I could sneak into heaven without anyone noticing."

Anyway, I told Wil about Thomas Burgess's suggestion, and before the evening Wil's plan was ready. One of the spinners, Jac Jones by name, always wore a top hat, and placed it on a nail outside the spinning-room. Wil's plan was to tie a fine, black thread around the base of the hat, by the brim, and take it in a quarter-inch, and a quarter-inch, as you know, is two sizes on a hat, and then to persuade Jac Jones that his head had swollen. The plan delighted old Burgess. The next morning, as soon as Jac Jones had gone to his work, Wil neatly tied the thread around the hat, and, according to the plan, I went into the spinning-room, and said to Jac:

"John Jones, aren't you well today?"

"I am, my boy, why did you ask?"

"Oh, nothing," I said, "only that I think there is some swelling in your temples."

"No, there isn't, *neno dyn*[1], I'm in excellent health, thankfully," said Jac.

About seven o'clock Wil went to him, and said:

"John Jones, you don't look as you usually do this morning; do you have a headache?"

---

[1] '*neno dyn*' or '*yn enw dyn*' in full, translates literally as '*in man's name*' there is little doubt that the use of the word '*man*' used to swear an oath here, is not invoking the witness of any ordinary '*man*', but the '*Son of Man*', that is, Jesus, the Son of God.

"Dear me, I don't; but Ned was asking the same thing earlier; what made you think that?"

"I don't know," said Wil, "but there's something odd-looking about your head, as if you've had a blow on one side. Let me see the other side. No, both sides are the same; must be my imagination, I suppose," and off Wil went to his work.

Some five minutes before breakfast time, old Burgess went to him and said:

"Here you are, Jac, were you in some fight last night? You've been boozing at the old drink again, because your head's like a round turnip; or have you caught the mumps that are going around just now?"

"I haven't touched a drop for a week, and my head is as good as any of your heads," said Jac curtly.

"I hope you're telling the truth," said Burgess, and off he went.

When Jac was going to his breakfast, and trying to put his hat upon his head, for the life of him he couldn't. He checked to see if he had taken someone else's hat, but remembered that nobody wore a top hat but himself, and his name, written in his own hand, was inside it. He borrowed a cap to go to his breakfast, and carried the hat in his hand. John Jones didn't come to his work after breakfast. At mid-day Burgess visited him, and found him in his bed, suffering tremendous pains in his head. Burgess told Jac that it was the mumps, without a doubt, but that a remedy had been discovered to treat them instantly, and that he would bring it to him that afternoon, after the mill closed. Burgess and I visited Jac that evening, and took with us some sweet oil in a bottle. While Burgess and Jac's wife were upstairs administering the oil to his head, I was in the kitchen removing the thread from the hat; and in order to demonstrate how effective the remedy was, Burgess sent Jac's wife to fetch the hat, and Jac was able to put it on his head with ease. In fact, with so much oil on his head, the hat slipped on rather too easily, and it was as well that Jac had rather large ears to prevent it from covering his face. But strangely, the pain did not subside immediately, although the swelling disappeared straight away, and Jac Jones was on the club benefit for a week before returning to work. He wasn't told about the trick for three weeks, and he never forgave us.

Here's another, similar enough, story for you, said my Uncle Edward, but I'll tell that one later perhaps.

7

EDWARD CWM TYDI

As a partner to the story about Jac Jones and his hat, here's another story for you that shows how easy it is to cure some men of a serious illness, and the story's true, every word—I knew the people, and there are others still alive who knew them. What made me remember the story was hearing about the Sequa[1] that goes about the country curing people of rheumatism in minutes by rubbing them.

About sixty years ago, there lived on a smallholding called Cwm Tydi, near Llangollen, a brother and sister, a bachelor and a spinster called Edward and Ann. In those days people were known by the places they lived in, or by the professions they followed. Although I knew the brother and sister well, I didn't know them by any name other than Edward and Ann Cwm Tydi. The bachelor and the spinster were quite old. Edward was a big, strong and healthy man, but his sister Ann was somewhat frail.

Once, Edward was taken very ill with rheumatism, so that he could barely move in his bed, or suffer anyone to touch him, and he was in great pain, and in haste Doctor Morris from Llangollen was called for. The doctor was a curt, concise man, and on hearing of Edward's illness he came to Cwm Tydi immediately, and said that he would send a bottle of medicine to the patient. Doctor Morris had a servant called Wil, a boy from Llantysilio, who looked after his horses, and who sometimes helped the doctor to mix the medicine. I never heard a name for this boy except Wil, the Doctor's lad. Wil was a pure and mischievous Welshman, and I remember him well. After preparing the bottle, the Doctor

---

[1] *Sequa* is a word used to describe someone of dark complexion, perhaps a gypsy.

told Wil to write on it that it would need shaking well before the medicine was given to the patient. Wil wrote: *He must be well shaken before taken*, putting '*he*' instead of '*it*'. Whether this was from mischief or ignorance, I don't know.

When the bottle reached Cwm Tydi, neither Ann nor Edward could understand a word of the instruction, for they hadn't had an hour's schooling in their lives. There was at Cwm Tydi a servant-lad called Abram who had had some education, and he was called into the patient's room 'to read the bottle', so that they might know how the medicine was to be taken. Abram told Ann:

"We have to shake him well before giving him the medicine."

"Shake him?"

"Yes," said Abram, "It says on the bottle: *He must be well shaken before taken*."

"I can't shake him, I'm too weak," said Ann.

"We have to, because the bottle says so," said Abram, and Edward groaned in his bed.

"Well," said Ann, "as the Doctor says we must, we'll have to."

The bedclothes were thrown off Edward, and Abram went one side of the bed and Ann the other, and they shook Edward well, until they were drenched with sweat, and Edward was crying blue murder. Edward lost his voice from yelling so hard, and Ann and Abram thought he was about to die. The two sat down, short of breath, to wait and see if Edward would recuperate. Presently Edward asked:

"Abram, how often does the bottle say I must be shaken?"

"Three times a day," said Abram.

"Ho," said Edward, "I'll have none of that regime," and he got up slowly and dressed himself, and felt quite well.

The next day Doctor Morris came to Cwm Tydi, and was met at the top of the yard by Ann.

"How is Edward today, Ann?" said the Doctor.

"Well," said Ann, "I don't think the medicine did him much good, but the shaking did him the world of good. Abram and I shook him as hard as we could before giving him the medicine, like the bottle said, and in no time he got up and dressed himself without help, and today he's quite active."

Doctor Morris saw the mistake, and said:

"The reason I ordered him to be shaken well was to help him digest the medicine," and then he set off clutching his sides.

Later, Abram became a servant-lad with my father, and I once saw him eat a sieve-full of raw onions, but that's another story, said my Uncle Edward.

8

THOMAS OWEN, CHAPEL HOUSE

Whilst telling you the other night about William and Richard Bonner, I made some reference to Thomas Owen of Tŷ'r Capel in Mold. Thomas was one of the strangest characters I ever saw. He was a cobbler by trade, but also a preacher with the Methodists. You didn't often see men thinner than he, but he was quite effervescent and an excellent walker. His nose was exactly the same shape as the Duke of Wellington's, like a door-knocker. Talking of his nose reminds me of a comical thing that happened to it. Thomas had a tendency when preaching to hold out his index finger as if he was pointing at a member of the audience, and then he'd hold his nose between finger and thumb, and then the index finger would come out again. On one occasion the people of Nercwys had invited Thomas Owen to early-morning service in chapel at five o'clock in the morning, an invitation which he accepted enthusiastically enough. The chapel was packed. Neither lamps nor gas had come into use then. There'd be wax candles everywhere, and a set of snuffers on every pulpit so that the preacher could extinguish the candles when they began to dim. Thomas prayed fervently that morning, and that's the period when he was pleading on behalf of the queen of Madagascar. "Save her, Lord, or get rid of the ill-tempered old Jade," said Thomas. Anyway, as he was starting to preach, he noticed that the candles were beginning to dim, and he looked about him for the snuffers, but there weren't any. Thomas wet his finger and thumb on his lip and cut off the candle-heads. Then he held his nose, leaving a big sooty mark on it. The people began to laugh. Thomas became greatly agitated when he saw the congregation so jocular, and he reproved them sharply, and he held his nose for the second time until it was as black as his shoe, and the people laughed more and more, particularly the naughty lads. Eventually, Thomas said, "What's possessed you, you godless people? Such behaviour in the house of God is a disgrace to religion! If this is what early-morning service is, I shall never attend one again as long as I live," and he ended the sermon in a foul mood. But having understood the cause of the laughter and having seen his face in a mirror, he too laughed.

Thomas Owen was a native of Bala, and he was the son of Richard Owen, the man who prayed that Mr Charles's life should be extended by fifteen years and was answered, and it was during that period that Mr Charles composed the Dictionary that has been a priceless blessing for Wales[1]. Thomas was also greatly distinguished as a man of prayer, and some of his public entreaties were most evidently answered. Once, Thomas was preaching in Adwy'r Clawdd at a time of considerable poverty and hardship. Hundreds were out of work and suffering from lack of nourishment. Thomas earnestly and tenaciously prayed for the Lord to reveal some valuable seam in the neighbourhood that would bring work for his needy creatures, and said to Almighty God: "You, Lord, have plenty of wealth in this earth if you'd only direct someone's eye to where it is." Within two or three days a seam of lead was found which brought work to the whole area for years.

In those days news took a long time to travel, and Michael Roberts of Pwllheli, the famous preacher, had been in the asylum at Chester for some time before Thomas Owen came to hear of it, and when he heard he felt it to the quick. The following Monday evening, in the prayer meeting, Thomas, in his own way, earnestly and fervently prayed for the great man's restoration. He cried loudly and intensely: "Lord, remember dear little Meic! Remember your servant Meic," etc. Before the end of the week Michael Roberts was in Angel Jones's house in Mold, waiting for the stagecoach to

---

[1] Mr Charles is Thomas Charles (1755–1814), the leader of the second generation of Welsh Methodist Calvinists, a truly great organiser, teacher, author and publisher.

Rhuthun, and much restored to health. Angel mentioned Thomas Owen's prayer to him, and it was understood that Michael Roberts has his cure at exactly the same time as Thomas prayed.

Thomas Owen for a while manned a turnpike toll-gate in Gwernymynydd, and he was then very poor, but he was second-to-none in his attendance at chapel-services. Some of the brethren noticed his impoverished appearance, his cotton very mean and fraying, and some of them decided amongst themselves to present him with a new suit, and directed Angel Jones to make it. On Saturday evening Thomas quite proudly went home with his suit tucked under his arm, and on Sunday morning he put it on, and turned about for his wife Marged to examine it. "Will it do, Marged?" he said. "You look like a gentleman," she said. Thomas felt very pleased with the observation, and began his journey to the chapel. After going some twenty yards, he stopped suddenly to look at himself, and turned back. "What's wrong?" asked Marged. "Well to you, I won't go to chapel in these clothes," he said. "Why not?" said Marged. "I'll tell you why," said Thomas, "when people see these new clothes, everyone will say I'm stealing the toll-gate money." "Don't be silly," said Marged, "don't chapel people know that the suit is a present?" "They do," said Thomas, "but, you see, the people who are not chapel members don't know, and they'll say, 'Look at him, the old cobbler: the gate's paying well!' No, Marged, I won't wear these new clothes." Thomas removed the suit and jumped into his old scabby rags, and set off at a trot for Mold feeling ten times happier. It was he who was to preach in Mold that morning, and the generous brethren were disappointed when they saw him in his old clothes, but Thomas explained to them why that was, and nobody could persuade him to wear the suit until he had left the toll-gate and come to live in the chapel house in Mold.

While Thomas was manning the toll-gate at Gwernymynydd, Edward Roberts, probably one of the most able chapel elders that ever there was in Mold, lived a little further up than he in the same district. I have a faint memory of Edward Roberts, a man very similar in physique to Doctor Edwards of Bala, only shorter. Edward Roberts and Jones, Cefn y Gader, Glan Alun's father, were considered the two strongest pillars of the church in Mold. Edward Roberts, Gwernymynydd was a slow, cautious and scholarly man, and his opinion amongst the brethren the last word on every subject. Thomas Owen was frail, impulsive, and sprightly as a sparrow. No two men more dissimilar ever wore breeches, and yet they were great friends. Edward would never go to a service or meeting without calling at the gate for Thomas Owen. One *seiat*-evening a point of doctrine was under discussion, and Thomas and Edward differed greatly in their opinions. The debate was carried on between the two along the road to Gwernymynydd, and Thomas had become so incensed and Edward so furious that they didn't say good night to each other. Thomas would take offence in a minute and would make peace within a minute. Edward Roberts did not often take offence, but when he did take offence he'd remain offended. The next Sabbath-morning, Thomas said to Marged, "Let's see if old Ned calls here today. He'd gone right into his shell on Thursday evening, but let's see if he's come to. If he passes, let him—don't go to the door. Here he comes, pretty straight, full of the old Adam, I'll warrant! Don't get into view, Marged, let's see what he does."

The gatehouse was in the middle of a cluster of houses, and Edward went on his way through the gate without calling for Thomas. But he hadn't gone ten yards before Thomas had run to the door and put his hands to his mouth and made a trumpet of them, and hollered at the top of his voice:

"Ho! ho!! ho!!! There goes an old elder to chapel without having said his prayers!" The whole neighbourhood got up and Edward Roberts turned back in embarrassment, and Thomas and he were better friends than ever.

I was told the next story about Thomas Owen by Dr Roger Hughes of Bala. Years ago, a preacher would be invited to tour part of a county in order to help him pay the rent, and some other preacher would be invited because the country wished to hear him. Perhaps the people of Meirion were induced by more than one reason when they invited Thomas Owen on a preaching tour through a part of the county. Everyone who has studied geography knows that Merionethshire is divided into two parts by the Methodists, namely 'this end' and 'that end'. Although I've been to both ends more than once, I never found out which was 'this end' and which 'that end', because when I was in Harlech, the residents called Corwen 'that end', and when I was in Corwen the people called Harlech and its surrounding area 'that end'. Therefore I can't decide which end Thomas Owen toured. But it's pretty well-known that he visited Cwmtirmynach, and that he had there a remarkably difficult service, and nothing vexed Thomas Owen more than a difficult service, and he's lucky that he isn't alive these days. Ten years later Thomas Owen had another invitation to tour his native county. The first service was to be in Bala at ten o'clock in the morning, and he was notified that he would be informed of his itinerary once he got there. He was lent Jones Cefn-y-Gader's horse for the journey, and Thomas hoped all along the way that Cwmtirmynach wasn't on the list. After preaching in Bala, one of the elders passed him his itinerary, and much to his dismay he was to preach in Cwmtirmynach at two o'clock. Thomas said nothing, but decided in himself that he'd ride like Jehu past Cwmtirmynach chapel, and head for the place where he was to preach in the evening. When he was within about half a mile of the chapel he gave his horse some wind so that he could ride faster past the chapel. But some old woman on two walking-sticks came out from a cabin on the roadside, and said, "Well, Thomas Owen dear, and you've come! Bless you! It's been ten years since you were here last." "Ah," said Thomas, muttering to himself, "she remembers that difficult old service!" "If I ever felt conviction," the old woman added, "it was through that sermon that I came by it. I remember your text well enough—'He that spared not his own Son, but delivered him up for us all', etc. I'll never forget that wonderful service, Thomas Owen *bach*."

"What? What?" said Thomas, and, after further conversation with the old woman became convinced that she was telling the truth. He didn't ride past Cwmtirmynach, but had there the most successful service of his tour. What a comfort to the preachers of difficult services! said my Uncle Edward.

9

THE MINISTER

Did I know James Lewis? Indeed I did, said my Uncle Edward. And I never think of him without feeling a wave of sadness cross my soul. James was an unusual man. His parents were Methodists, and James was their only child. Dafydd Lewis kept a food shop. The shop was but a small one, and although Dafydd was diligent and respected among his neighbours, he was always struggling to make ends meet. Ever since I was a boy I used to look upon James Lewis as one possessing more talent than all the boys of the area put together. He was so bright as a boy that many prophesied that he would grow dull as he grew older. When four years old he amazed everyone by reciting verses and stanzas. Naturally enough his father and mother thought the world of him. Praise his father's heart, he gave James the best school that he could, of the sort of schools that were in those days. I heard my father say many times that he was sure Dafydd was putting himself under great pressure to provide Jim *bach*, as he called him, with an education. It's strange, and a mercy, how things have changed. You'll never have seen how people, and pretty good people too, blamed Dafydd Lewis. Some said that it was his pride entirely, others said that he was leading his son to the gallows by giving him so much schooling, and others quite spitefully said that shop-keeping must be paying well. Little did they know that Dafydd had to borrow money many times from my father to pay the rent in order to meet James's school costs. But that's how it was; and some people's jealousy and foolishness were so great that they never went to Dafydd Lewis's shop to spend a penny if they could avoid it.

Despite all the prophesying that James the shop would grow dull, the lad continued to improve and shine. He was a peerless learner;

but his earnest desire was to be able to speak English well, and that in those days was great scholarship. Indeed, upon hearing the ten-year old James speak English smoothly and fluently, we the boys looked upon him as some kind of second Dic Aberdaron[1]. Books were scarce in the area, and when James went to neighbours' houses and saw there a book he had not read, he was not allowed to borrow it even when he asked—people were so jealous. This made him borrow the books without asking, and he was given the reputation of a book-thief. But it was to satisfy his soul that he turned thief.

After James had finished his schooling, he went to help his father in the shop, but he would spend more time reading than helping, and he would never refuse a customer credit, thereby, it is said, adding a lot to the shop account book. As talented boys generally are, he was full of fun and innocent mischief. This made the elders watch him carefully and frown upon him. There were held in those days what was called a children's *seiat*, and looking back on those meetings I must say that the main aim of Pitar Bellis, the man who led these meetings, was to suppress James Lewis, by preventing him from reciting too many verses, or parts of sermons—pressing James down to the other children's level, rather than raising them up to James's level. Thinking about Pitar Bellis's cruel words, it amazes me to think how the boy came there at all. "Don't be such a blabber-mouth, my lad, show some restraint while reciting the sermon, won't you, don't be so quick with your answer, wait until I ask you," and suchlike words were the mildest comments poor James would be given. It was a long time before he was accepted as a full member of the chapel, while others younger and as dull as gateposts were accepted long before he was, and the biggest complaint they had against him was that he combed his hair off his forehead and put

---

[1] Dic Aberdaron, or, to give him his proper name, Richard Robert Jones (1780–1843), had the reputation of being a polyglot: it is said that he could learn the classics and modern languages at the drop of a hat. But during his peripatetic life as a sort of super-tramp he had little or no use for them and little or no interest in their literatures.

oil in it. That, at that time, was a greater crime than not knowing the *Hyfforddwr*[2]. James could recite the *Hyfforddwr* from start to finish, and was an honourable and kind boy, but this counted for nothing with the old brethren—he had a QP, and he was too much of a blabber-mouth, as Pitar Bellis would say. And it was as if from shame, seeing that he was such a tall lad, that he was eventually admitted. James established a meeting for the young boys, and although nothing worse happened in them than speechmaking, reading and recitation competitions, the elders soon put a stop to it. However, in secret, we had many meetings in Dafydd Lewis's warehouse, which contained not only reading and speechmaking, but the occasional sermon given by James, sometimes in Welsh, other times in English. We had a greater regard for the English sermon because we didn't understand it.

To get to the point, rumour spread that James could preach very well, and he could too. A few of the church-members believed James had been born to be a preacher—he was witty, knowledgeable, and physically handsome, and his character was unblemished, and when he was about eighteen years old some tried to put his case forward, and he himself was eager for that. But there was no chance that the old fathers in the elders' pew would agree—they wanted to take things more steadily. And that's how things were for James Lewis for about two years—he was looked upon as one intended to preach, but unable to get a license. In those days the Welsh Independents had a young minister—an acceptable man who had had a better education than most ordinary preachers. He and James became friends, and before long James asked for his membership token so that he could join the Independents. Everyone opened their eyes—they saw their mistake, but it was too late. I well remember that some of us, his chief companions, were distraught at the thought of our witty and kind friend leaving us, and amongst ourselves we

---

[2] *Yr Hyfforddwr* was a catechism written by the same Thomas Charles mentioned in a previous note.

were not short of attacking the old brethren. Within a few weeks James was preaching enthusiastically with the Independents, in Welsh and in English, he didn't mind which, and he was spoken of throughout the country as one of the most promising young men the denomination possessed.

This went on for quite a time when a family of Englishmen from London, who were Independents, came to the neighbourhood for a month, for their health. They heard James preach, and were enamoured of him. Within a few months of the family's return, James was invited to London on supply, as is said. He went and stayed there. Shortly afterwards, we heard that he had been confirmed as the minister of a flourishing church, that the appointment was a happy one, and that he was getting along excellently.

Twelve years passed, and in the meantime we would hear occasionally about James's success and popularity. But one day, who did we see in the neighbourhood but James. He looked respectable, but there was something very different in him compared to how he normally looked. He was grave and quiet, and it was obvious that something unpleasant had happened to him, and for that reason no-one questioned him. We understood directly that he did not intend to return to London. By now his parents had been dead for some time, but, as it happened, the shop that they had rented was empty, and we were very surprised when word went out that James had taken his father's old shop, which he opened immediately. He would go to the Independent chapel on the Sabbath, but we understood that he didn't stay for the fellowship, or, as we call it, the *seiat*. He and the minister, who had started him out as a preacher, appeared to be quite friendly, and many believed that only Mr Price knew the reason why James had abandoned the ministry, and re-establish a business, but people conjectured a lot. The business in the shop was paltry, but it was thought that James didn't want for anything. Things continued like this for a long time, and I was quite friendly with James and would visit his shop from time to time, but I had never asked him for an explanation for his leaving London, for I knew he had refused to explain to many. I was in the shop one evening when the lad was putting up the shutters, and, for the first time since he had returned, he invited me into the house. We were old friends, and would call each other *ti* and *tithau*.[4] After reminiscing about the old days for some time, I dared to ask him why he had abandoned the ministry. He looked at me as if I'd shot him, then put his head between his hands on the table and cried terribly. I saw that I'd hurt him, and regretted asking the question. After he had composed himself, he answered as follows, as far as I can remember:

"Edward, you and I are old friends, and I know, if I ask you, that won't repeat what I'm about to say, as long as I'm alive, do as you will afterwards. So that you don't think it's anything worse, here's the story in brief. You know that I was confirmed in a comparatively flourishing church in London. At first I was pretty worried that I lacked the resources for the job. I worked hard and tirelessly late into the night and early in the morning, and soon I felt that God was blessing me and acknowledging my labours. The church improved and the adherents increased greatly. There were six deacons—good and gracious men, and we cooperated excellently. Things went on like this for years without a hitch. There belonged to our church a spinster—not much older than myself—who was rich and influential. She was everything except beautiful. She was considered the most religious of us all—she would never miss a service on the Sabbath or during the week. She would visit the poor regularly, and some of them were almost entirely dependent on her. She was our Dorcas. She contributed to the ministry and to other causes as much as a dozen of the most generous people, and there was no end to her generosity to me, the minister. Besides that, she had had a good education, and was very intelligent. It's easy for you to believe that her influence in the church was vast. Indeed, we wouldn't dream of embarking on any project without first consulting Miss Perks— that was her name—for we knew that we would have to rely on

---

[3] '*Ti*' and '*tithau*' are second person singular and familiar forms of address.

her purse, and that she would never begrudge us, for she was, as I believed, a saint, as well as rich. As minister, I was expected to visit every member of the church in turn, but naturally enough, as you can imagine, I fell into the habit of visiting Miss Perks much more often than anyone else, for I could spend an hour or two in her company to my own advantage. Very often she would have a new book, and if she had read it, I'd get it as a gift. I valued her above all others. This went on for eleven years, and everyone knew that I visited her often, more often than I should have, perhaps. In the twelfth year of my ministry Miss Perks began to deride me because I wasn't married; I told her that I had no time to think of marrying. She continued to deride me every time I went there, until I tired of her story, and began to visit her less often. One day I was invited there for tea, and I went, for it didn't do to disobey Miss Perks. After tea, she told me, with considerable feeling, that she had set her mind upon me as a husband, and that she would not be refused. I took fright, for, although I thought very highly of her, marrying her was the last thing on my mind. I told her that I was very grateful to her for her kind offer, but that I had never thought about marrying; and she answered that it was high time for me to think, and that's how the conversation ended. The next time I went there she brought the subject up once again, and gave me an account of her assets, and she said that she'd transfer all of it to me if I married her; but I changed the subject, trying to laugh it off, although I didn't feel like laughing, and I soon left. The subject was broached again on my next visit, and I told her that if she referred to it again I would have to stop visiting her, and she responded that she would continue to talk until I listened to her. I didn't go there again. By now I was wretched, and knew that the predicament was having an effect on my preaching—I was thoroughly uneasy, and couldn't get my thoughts together in preparation for the Sabbath—Miss Perks in her pew in the chapel was in the forefront of my mind all the time. I had no idea what to do. I wished in my heart for a call to some other church, which I'd had more than once when I was not ready to take it. One evening I was surprised to see the six deacons in the church meeting—that was a rarity, for they were busy men, full of their problems with the world. After the meeting, in the vestry-room, I could tell from their faces that something was wrong, and without my going into the details for you, they said that they had a serious complaint against me—that Miss Perks had informed them that I had on more than one occasion behaved indecently towards her, and in a manner entirely inappropriate for a minister of the Gospel, and that, of course, they could not doubt Miss Perks's word. I was amazed, and something came into my throat so that I couldn't say a word for some time, and I was shaking like a leaf. I was awfully angry with myself, for I knew that they looked upon these signs as evidence of my guilt. When I came to, I told them what I've told you already. But I knew that they didn't believe me, and they told me that what I had reported was unlike Miss Perks—that they'd known her for thirty years. The eldest deacon—the wisest and best of them—said that they had consulted each other, and that the best thing for me, for the great cause, and for the church, was to resign at once: that they had come to this decision with great grief, but that they had to consider Miss Perks's feelings. After a great deal of talking, and after I had made many a vow, I shook hands with them all, and there wasn't one dry face. I rushed to my lodgings like a madman, and came here the very next day. You can imagine my state of mind ever since then. But I pray day and night for God to clear my name, and I believe He will one day, perhaps after I've departed this earth. Nobody here knows the story except for Mr Price the Independent minister, and he's pleaded with me several times to investigate the case, but I've stopped him. Keep everything to yourself for now."

James Lewis and I were better friends than ever after this. Three years later I called into his shop one day, and his assistant told me that Mr Lewis had gone away for a few days. Before the end of that week I received a word from him to go there. He was cheerful, but terribly excited. He showed me a document reporting Miss Perks's deathbed confession that she had told an absolute untruth about her 'dear minister'. While dying, the old vixen had felt the heat of the eternal fire and found it too hot, and had urged the deacons to summon James Lewis. She made her confession in front of James and four of the deacons, and with her last breath, as it were, she tried to make him accept some financial compensation for the wrong, but James scornfully refused that. But James told me that he'd forgiven her, and that he'd prayed at her bedside for God to forgive her. Miss Perks died the next day, and James returned with a clear character and a clear conscience. But the predicament affected him so severely that he too died not long afterwards. And that's James Lewis's story for you, one of the most talented boys I ever saw, and the story's as true as the Lord's Prayer, said my Uncle Edward.

10

WILLIAM THE SHEPHERD

Remember William the shepherd's story? Of course I do, as if it had happened yesterday, said my Uncle Edward. And it's a strange story, too. William was one of the handsomest men you ever saw: more than two yards in height, and of strong and sturdy constitution. He was also regarded by his neighbours as one of the bravest and most fearless men one could meet in a year. This was fortunate for William, for his occupation sometimes required him to be on the mountains at any time of night, and in all kinds of weather. William was in truth a shepherd, and if there was something wrong with the sheep, the severity of the weather didn't make him neglect them. He endangered his life tens of times to rescue an old ewe or a lamb that in themselves were worth nothing. And it's my belief that God takes kindly upon a man for such things—there is something divine in risking life to save life.

Well, William was in love with the daughter of Yr Henblas[1], and was about to get married. And Susan Yr Henblas was a very lovely girl, I remember her well, and after William had set his heart upon her no-one else dared to think of her in fear of William, for, as I said, William was a wonderfully strong man, although, for all I heard, he was totally harmless, and I never heard that he got drunk or used foul language. There were three miles or more from the village where William lived to Yr Henblas, and the road was over the mountain. But William would go to visit Susan two or three times every week, regardless of the weather.

---

[1] *'Henblas'*, *'Hen'* means *'old'*, *'Plas'* comes from the English *'palace'*, but in Wales the word will often refer to a humbler abode. *'Yr'* is the definite article *'the'*.

One evening there was to be a midweek service in the chapel, and almost every time there was something in chapel on a weekday evening, it was customary for us, the sons and servants of farmers, to go to the chapel a quarter of an hour or so before the service, to talk amongst ourselves and hear the news. The custom met with some disapproval, but there was something to be said for it—seldom did we see each other except on such occasions, for we lived so far apart. Well, like I said, there was to be a service in the chapel on Wednesday evening, and several us young men had assembled at the chapel in advance. It was a frosty night, and quite light, and after we had been talking for some time, who did we see coming toward us from the direction of the mountain but William the shepherd. When he reached us we all noticed that he looked agitated, and I asked him if something had happened to the sheep, and he said—and here is his every word:

"No, nothing, Edward, but you know what, I saw something awfully strange as I came over that ridge. You know that I'm not afraid, but when I was coming down that hillside I came suddenly to pitch blackness—I couldn't see my hand. I wasn't frightened, and I went on through the darkness and then I came into the light, and I stood to look back, and I could see a black, long, low cloud, and flat on top like the top of a wall or a hedge cut level. Whilst continuing to look at it I could see, after a bit, a crowd of people like a procession on the other side of the cloud. Only their heads and shoulders were visible to me, and although it appeared they were almost next to me I didn't recognise any of them. I saw the people moving forward and the cloud too, and then I noticed that four men at the front of the cloud were carrying a coffin on a bier, and there was one man behind the bier on horseback, and I recognised him immediately—it was John Roberts Y Foty[2], on his black horse. I stood to watch until the cloud and the people

---

[2] '*Foty*' is an abbreviation of '*Hafod-tŷ*'. '*Tŷ*' means house; '*Hafod*', as has been explained before, refers to a highland farmstead occupied during the summer months.

went across the river along the road to the church, until I lost sight of them."

William's story was very strange to all of us, and to him himself more than anyone, and we believed every word of the story, because William the shepherd was a perfectly truthful man. Seeing him so agitated, I frivolously told him that the vision was a premonition of his wedding, and we went into the chapel and William with us. But the strangest thing is yet to come. Within a week of that Wednesday evening it had been snowing quite heavily, but true to his engagement William the shepherd crossed the mountain to Yr Henblas to visit Susan. He did not stay long with his beloved, for he remembered about the journey home he had on such a night. Soon, after he had left Yr Henblas, it began to snow heavily, and he turned into a tavern to wait for the snow-shower to pass. He had only one glass—he would never take more than one—for William was a moderate and very sober man. Seeing that it was still snowing, he decided to head for home—he was perfectly familiar with the mountain, and had been on it tens of times in worse weather, he said. But William never reached his home alive. He was found the next day dead in the snow. Now the youngsters remembered William's story by the chapel gate, and we wondered at the thought of it. Within a few days I, and several of the youngsters who had listened to his story, were at his funeral, and we could barely hold our breath when we saw no-one on horse-back other than John Roberts Y Foty. Shortly after this, Susan Yr Henblas broke her heart, and she died of consumption.

How you explain a story like William the shepherd's, I don't know, but it's as true as I'm sitting in this chair, and there are quite a few alive today who remember it as well as I do, said my Uncle Edward.

11

HUGH BURGESS'S DOG

My Uncle Edward said:

I've mentioned to you before Thomas Burgess, the foreman in the cotton factory in Mold. His wife was a bit younger than he, and they had one child, a boy of about nine years old. Although, as I have said, Thomas Burgess was a quite cruel man, he was very fond of his son, and pampered him excessively, and so did Mrs Burgess. Indeed, many believed that old Burgess and his wife had no other purpose in life but the contentment and pleasure of their son Hugh. Hugh's great delight was dumb animals, and through his parents' generosity he had in the house a variety of birds, and in the yard pigeons, rabbits, a small mule, and I don't know how many other things, and the other boys of the area envied him the multitude of his livestock. Hugh attended the British School, which was about a mile from his home, and so that he didn't have to walk back and forth he took his lunch with him to school in a pretty little basket.

Opposite the British School, you know, in one of those tiny houses, lived a man called Martin, who earned his living—honestly enough, for all I know—by selling nuts, oranges, India rock and the like, and he would frequently visit the markets in Rhuthun, Denbigh and Wrexham. Martin was an Irishman, and had a little light cart on four wheels, its top flat as a table, to carry his goods to the markets, and it served him as a stall. The little cart would be pulled by two large dogs, and going downhill Martin would jump on top of the cart, and the dogs would go like lightning. But Martin would have to help them uphill. I wondered a hundred times at the strength and ready obedience of Martin's dogs. He had three of them, and the oldest was called Sam.

Sam had worked diligently on the hard roads for many years, and had grown old, and you know that a decade is a century for a dog. But Sam was twelve years old, and one day he became terribly lame and was no longer able to pull the cart. Sam was an invalid in Martin's kennel for weeks, and Hugh Burgess would take some of his lunch to him every day he was at school, and the two became firm friends. Martin had no hope that Sam would improve sufficiently to be able to take up pulling the cart again, and so did not give him half enough food, and if it wasn't for Hugh Burgess, Sam would have starved long since. One mid-day when Hugh was taking some of his lunch to Sam, he saw Martin heading to the yard before him, with a gun under his arm. Hugh ran and asked Martin what he was going to do.

"Shoot Sam," said Martin, "because he'll never be good for anything again."

Hugh burst into tears, and pleaded to be allowed to take Sam home with him, a plea that was immediately granted, for Martin was glad to get the old dog off his hands. Sam seemed to understand the discussion between Hugh and Martin, for when his old master turned his back, taking the gun with him to the house, he wagged his tail, as if a great load had been lifted from his mind. Sam had seen several of his companions being shot after becoming too lame to pull the cart. That evening Hugh took Sam home with him, and the old dog made considerable effort to follow him on his three legs.

Gentle as Hugh's parents were, the boy got a harsh telling-off for bringing such a big, pawed, hairy, famished creature near to the house, and old Burgess insisted on shooting the dog immediately. But Hugh knew about his father's weakness, and began to wail bitterly. Hugh was permitted to turn out the little mule, and give his pen to Sam, and by now, seeing the dog walking on his three legs, old Burgess playfully said:

"It's easy to see that the poor creature's been living by the school."

"How so?" said Mrs Burgess.

"Because he's learned simple addition—three down, carry one," said Burgess.

Through a considerable amount of care, kindness, and plenty of food, Sam recovered wonderfully, but his leg never got better. Every night after Hugh had returned from school, Sam could be seen following him sluggishly along the roads. In those days there was a very pretty little boat on the big factory lake, but nobody was allowed to touch it apart from the factory owner and the foreman and their families. Hugh had learned to row the boat very skilfully. One summer evening Burgess and his wife and Hugh went for a walk towards the lake, with Sam hobbling at their heels. Hugh insisted on showing his father and mother how skilfully he could handle the boat. His mother objected, for it was getting dark.

"Let him," said Burgess, and Hugh easily pushed the boat from the shore.

When he was in the middle of the lake, old Burgess watched him with admiring eyes, and said:

"He'll be quite a chap, if he lives."

No sooner had he said this than Hugh lost hold of the oar, and it fell over the boat's side into the deep water. His father and mother shouted in frenzy, but nobody was within earshot to help them. At the same moment the old dog leapt into the water, but his wounded leg so hindered him he could only swim badly. Hugh's head appeared, and disappeared again, and thus two or three times, whilst poor Sam tried his best to reach him. They lost sight of the dog and the boy, and Mrs Burgess began to tear her clothes, without knowing what she was doing. But in a minute they could see Sam's head above the water, and he was heading toward the shore, and as if he were dragging something behind him, and looking exactly as he had done years ago when pulling the cart—his head held high, and batting his ears to keep away the insects. Soon he was close enough to Burgess for him to see that he had something between his teeth—yes, it was Hugh's jacket, and Hugh was being dragged to the shore by Sam. Having got the boy on to dry land it was some time before he came to; and Sam, if somebody had been noticing him, having shaken the water from his long hair, was watching Hugh's recuperation as anxiously as anyone. But poor Sam in his old age, he had done more than he was capable of that evening. He couldn't walk home. A handcart was fetched from the factory in order to transport him, but Sam died before the morning. Hugh almost broke his heart after the dog, and the neighbours said that they couldn't tell what was most obvious in old Burgess, his joy at his son's rescue, or his grief for Sam's death. That event did a deal of good to the foreman—he was gentler towards everyone from then on. He made an oak coffin for Sam, and buried him in the garden, and marked his grave with a stone. I don't know whether the stone is still there, said my Uncle Edward.

12

DOGS

The other night I was telling you about Hugh Burgess's dog. Dogs are strange animals, but a man who doesn't like a dog is a dog of a man. Mark you what I say to you now—if you see a man with a hatred for dogs, you'll find that such a man is not of the best sort, to say the least. Anyway, here's another story for you that's as true as the Lord's Prayer.

Many years ago, there lived in the Vale of Clwyd, near Llandyrnog, a husband and wife called, if I remember well, Pitar and Marged Jones. They rented a well-tended little farm, and were doing well. They had one son who hadn't the slightest inclination towards farming, and who was placed for a term in a shop in Rhuthun. The boy constantly desired to go to England, and at last was given a position in one of the shops owned by the munificent gentleman, Mr Tate, Liverpool, the sugar refiner. This boy had an uncle, his father's brother, who was a ship's captain, trading between Liverpool and the foreign countries, and when he returned from his journeys he'd usually have some present for the boy. Once, on his return from the distant lands, the captain brought his nephew a Newfoundland puppy. At that time the dog was no bigger than a hare. The boy 'lived out', as is said, that is, in lodgings, and thought the world of the little dog, and fed it and cared for it as well as he could for his uncle, the captain's sake. He wrote, of course, to his parents in the Vale of Clwyd telling them of the precious gift he'd received from his uncle. The boy's wages were small, and the dog ate everything that was put before it, and grew into a beautiful, huge creature, almost as big as a lion. After paying for his food and lodging, every halfpenny the boy had left went to feed the Newfoundland, and he didn't have a penny for the collection in chapel. The dog was eating him alive, and yet he wouldn't give it up for anything in the world, because it was his uncle's gift. He didn't know what to do. But eventually he decided to take it with him when he next went home, and that he'd leave the dog there, because his parents would have no trouble keeping it. The boy got permission to go home on Friday, with an order to return on Monday, and he took Lion with him—that was the dog's name. Everyone doted on the dog, and his paws were exactly like a lion's, and on the Saturday and Sunday Lion received a great deal of attention. Monday arrived, when he boy had to return on the first train, and he tied Lion up in one of the stables. Before setting off for Liverpool that morning, the boy changed his trousers, and left his old trousers folded tidily on a chair in the room in which he had slept. Sometime in the afternoon Lion was set free. He looked here and there for the boy, but, of course, he was by now in Liverpool. After searching every nook and cranny Lion went to the bedroom where the boy had slept, took the trousers that had been left on the chair in his mouth, and set off despite everyone. Before nightfall, Lion had reached the shop where the boy served, at the top of James Street, Liverpool, with the trousers in his mouth. And the dog and the trousers were perfectly dry. It was believed that Lion had waited for the packet steamer to cross to Birkenhead, and that, quite shamelessly, he had crossed the river without a ticket. When Mr Tate heard the dog's story, he bought him from the boy, and it remained in his possession for many years.

Here's another story for you. I think I've told you before that I'm acquainted with the family of Mr Roberts, Queen's Road, Liverpool. Mr Roberts died relatively young, leaving a widow and a number of children behind, but in a pretty comfortable position. This family also had some relative who traded with the distant lands, and he also brought back a Newfoundland dog for one of the children. Sultan, if I remember, was his name, and there was something in the dog's manner that was so grand and regal that his name suited him well. No-one had seen any tendency to cruelty in him, and if small dogs barked at him he would look at them with a noble contempt. The family thought so highly of him that he would be allowed to lie on the mat in front of the fire in the parlour, no matter who was present. Sultan was respected by the many preachers who used to visit Mrs Roberts, and he knew all the Methodist ministers in Liverpool, being particularly friendly with Henry Rees[1]. When Sultan went with one of the family down town, if they happened to meet Mr Rees, Sultan would put his cold nose in his hand, and the man of God would say—"Well, Sultan *bach*, how are you today? If there was ever a dog's soul within the circle of deliverance, I think for sure that you're the one who's got it," and Sultan with his great eyes would look into the minister's bright eyes, as if to say, "Thank you, Mr Rees."

But one of the greatest friends of the dear family in Queen's Road was Mr E. P——, an elder in the chapel of which they were members. Mr P—— would visit them two or three times every week, and he and Sultan were firm friends. One evening, Mr P—— was visiting, and Sultan was a great lump lying on the mat as usual, and half-closing his eyes, and the whole family was at home. But that evening Mr P—— had a walking stick in his hand, something the family had never seen him with before, and whilst he was shaking hands with Mrs Roberts and the children before sitting down, one of the girls began to tease him, saying that he was getting old, and had to have a stick. In jest, Mr P—— raised the stick above her head as if to strike her, when Sultan leapt up, and rushed at his throat upending him on the floor, and if the whole family had not taken hold of the dog, there's no doubt that it would have torn him to shreds. Sultan had thought that Mr P—— was going to hit the girl, and that moment had leapt to defend her. It was with great difficulty that the dog was brought to the back yard,

---

[1] Henry Rees (1798–1869), a native of Llansannan, Denbighshire, a greatly gifted preacher, who in 1864 became the first President of the General Assembly of the Calvinistic Methodists.

and Mr P—— and the family were terribly frightened. From that moment on, Sultan was chained in the back yard, and what was strange was this, that when Mr P—— came to the house, even though he'd come through the front door, the dog would instantly know that he was there, and rabidly try to get free. This made Mr P—— keep away from there, indeed, he was terrified to go into the street. Rather than lose Mr P——'s company, Sultan was shot, difficult as that was considering its faithfulness.

Here's another, stranger story for you, but true enough, for I heard the people themselves telling it, and this too was in Liverpool. You knew Foulkes *bach*, the tailor? Well, Foulkes had a sister who'd married a common labourer in Liverpool, and they lived in a street where there were many labourers' houses, and some distance from the docks. Jones was the man's name. They lived comfortably enough for some years, but were putting nothing away. Eventually business became bad, and Jones was thrown out of work. He was idle for some weeks, and he and his wife were almost starving. Jones went out every day to look for work, and returned time and again with an empty stomach and an empty pocket, except on those occasions when he had happened to come across an old friend and been given a few pence by him. He had done this for so long that he had truly tired of life, and he told the wife one day, when they didn't have a penny in the house, nor a dewdrop to eat—"I'll not go out again: I'll die by the fireside." His wife begged him to make one further attempt, saying to him as encouragement, that he might meet a friend, even if he did not get work. After some urging, Jones went out again, for the last time, or so he believed. He went along one street and then another, and whilst he went along the third, he noticed that a large fine-looking dog was following him. He tried to send the dog back, but it wouldn't go—it followed him everywhere he went. Before long a Welshman met him—a Welshman who looked like a sailor, who took a detailed look at the dog, and said: "Tell me, friend, is that dog for sale. And what's the price?" Jones did not know how to answer, in case the man owned the dog. But after considering for a moment, he said, "Well, it would be pretty difficult to part with the dog, but I'm very poor today." "I'll give you two pounds for him and say no more," said the man. "All right," said Jones. "My name is Captain Thomas, bring him to the ship *Margaret Ann* within an hour," said the Captain. And Jones did so, half in hope half in fear, and the two pounds were paid to him. When he was about to leave, the Captain asked, "What's its name?" "God-sent," said Jones. "A terribly strange name for a dog," said the sea-man. "An appropriate one, nonetheless," said Jones. Jones went home happily, and before the two pounds were spent he had found steady work. But here's the strangest part of the story—about ten months later, some time between seven and eight o'clock, Jones was eating his supper after returning from work, when he and his wife heard someone or something scratching at the door. His wife opened it, and in came God-sent, extraordinarily proud of himself. Of course, he received a warm welcome and plenty of food from Jones, but this was the first time his wife had seen the dog. Jones understood that the *Margaret Ann* was in the harbour, and having finished his meal and tidied himself up, he went to look for Captain Thomas. Having found the Captain, Jones told him the whole story, and he was amazed, but very glad to have the dog back again, and he gave Jones another sovereign, and said—"No wonder you named the dog God-sent, friend." I tell you that the story's perfectly true, though I don't know how to explain it. Perhaps the dog mistook Jones for his owner. But that seems unlikely. And how did it come by the street and the house where Jones lived the second time? I think most likely that God turned the dog's brain so that Jones and his wife could have a morsel and to keep them from starving.

13

TOMOS MATHIAS

By now, said my Uncle Edward, the old veterans of Waterloo have all gone, I suppose. I remember some of them well, and among them Tomos Mathias. Tomos lived in a tiny house behind the Blue Bell in Maesydref, Mold. Tomos's house was one of the smallest I ever saw in my life, and it's said that Jac, the carpenter, the owner of the house, built it one afternoon after finishing work and that Tomos received a letter in it the following morning. Regardless, it was the smallest house I ever saw. You could reach for everything that was in the kitchen without getting up from where you were sitting, and the bedchamber was only just big enough a space for a bed. People used to say, when Tomos was ill some time, that it was through the window that he showed his tongue to the doctor, who wanted to know the state of his stomach. But I don't know whether that was true or not. It was in this little cabin that Tomos and his wife Beti lived for many years. Tomos had been in a few battles, and in one of them—and I don't know whether that was at Waterloo—a bit of his skull was snatched away, a little above the crown. But the army's doctors did an amazingly neat job on the old man's head, by putting a silver plate over the hole lest his brain be visible. I saw the silver plate with my own eyes tens of times. Tomos would say that he was often without a penny, but never without silver. He received sixpence a day's pension for fighting for his country; but it was each quarter-year that he got the money from Sergeant-Major Evans. The major was a strange fellow, but that's another story.

Usually, Tomos was as happy as a cuckoo, and always as innocent as a dove. But he had in him one important vice—he was unusually fond of beer, and Beti was no teetotaller. As innocent as the two old heads were, they were frightful pagans, and they hadn't the first idea about religion. Tomos would attend church every three months—namely on the Sabbath before the pension was due, to remind the Sergeant-Major that he was alive. Tomos would receive credit to a certain sum from Mali Dafis, the little shop, and from one or two public houses, to await the day of the pension. Having reached the credit's limit, Tomos and Beti would be very poor. But the first thing the old soldier would do upon receiving his money—and in this he was an example to many in these days—was to go about to pay his debts, and then, more's the pity, he and Beti would spend the rest on beer. But, as I said, they would be hard up for weeks before the day of the pension, and Tomos would try many tricks in order to get a drop. On such an occasion, Tomos once went to a stranger who had just opened a pub in the neighbourhood, and asked:

"Good man, may I have a pint of beer from you?"

"Yes, if you've got the silver," said the publican.

"I'm never without silver," said Tomos, and the man handed him the drink. Upon seeing him make no sign of intent to pay, the publican said:

"Where's the brass, man?"

"I've no brass, but I've plenty of silver," said Tomos, and he removed his hat to show the man the silver plate on top of his head. The publican was greatly surprised, and didn't begrudge him for taking him for a ride.

One cold night in the winter, Tomos and Beti were shivering in front of a scrap of fire in the grate, and they were wildly famished, as it was but a week before the day of the pension. Beti sighed heavily, and said:

"You know what, Tomos, I wish I were in heaven."

"What did you say?" said Tomos.

"That I truly wish I were in heaven."

"Ho, is that so," said Tomos, "I myself wish I were in the pub with a pint of beer before me."

"You old scoundrel," said Beti, "you always wish for the best place."

I could relate for you a number of similar things about Tomos and Beti Mathias, said my Uncle Edward, but that's enough to show you how ignorant and harmless the old people were long ago, and how grateful you, the youngsters of this age, should be for your education and the Sunday School and its privileges.

14

THE GHOST OF THE CROWN

As Christmas draws near, said my Uncle Edward, I'm reminded of how people long ago would tell ghost stories by the fireside on long winter nights around this time of year. Education and the preaching of the Gospel have made a great change in Wales within my own memory, although I'm not very old. I remember when I was a young lad in Denbighshire that people generally believed in the appearance of ghosts, and I could name for you many places which they would say were haunted. Indeed, quite respectable people believed in their hearts that they had seen a ghost or something they couldn't explain. But your grandfather was a staunch Methodist, as you know, and his neighbours' superstition annoyed him greatly, and he went to considerable lengths with us to teach and enlighten us not to believe every ridiculous story about ghosts. By the time I was a young man, I believed that I wasn't the least bit afraid of all the ghosts in the world. But once I found that I wasn't as brave as I believed I was.

And this is how it was. My father and my Uncle Pitar were quite similar in their circumstances—they were fairly well-to-do, but money was generally scarce. There were fifteen miles between our house and Llwybr Main[1], the farm that Uncle Pitar rented. To meet some requirement, my father borrowed forty pounds from my uncle, and promised to repay them without fail on the twentieth of November, the day before the rent on Llwybr Main was due. My uncle definitely needed them to pay the rent, and the butcher who usually bought my father's sheep had promised to pay us fifty pounds a fortnight before the forty pounds were

---

[1] Llwybr Main: *the narrow path*.

wanted. But despite his promise, the butcher failed to keep his word, and my father had to explain his situation to him and press upon him, and he pledged to pay the money punctually.

Winter was early that year, with snow and ice on the ground days since. The twentieth of November came and the butcher hadn't shown his face, and my father had worried himself silly over the trouble he had caused my Uncle Pitar. But my mother said that the butcher was sure to come, and that we should be patient. It was afternoon and the butcher hadn't come, and my father insisted he'd never get a sheep from him again. But at about three o'clock the butcher came and paid the fifty pounds. By now my father was on tenterhooks thinking about my Uncle Pitar's anxiety, and I offered to take the money to Llwybr Main that evening. My father insisted that I go on horseback, but as I was keen to spend a few days at Llwybr Main I chose to walk there. It had begun to get dark before I started, and to shorten the journey I went over the mountain. I hadn't left home half an hour before it began to snow heavily. I walked and walked, and, to cut the story short, I lost my way. The snow was falling in huge flakes, and had made everywhere look strange to me, and I walked for hours without knowing where I was going, and the strangeness, the silence, and the fact that I had forty pounds in my pocket had made me quite nervous. But I had taken care to put a loaded revolver in the breast pocket of my coat, in case of thieves. I don't know how long I walked for, but I was exhausted, for you know that walking a mile in snow is more troublesome than walking three on dry land. I knew it was getting late, and because I was so tired I feared I might have to lie down in the snow, when I saw light like candlelight in a window, and I headed towards it. Having reached the light, I found that it came from the window of a small poor-looking house. I knocked on the door, and the man who lived there, who was about to go to bed, opened it, and directed me to the turnpike road. After reaching the turnpike I began to remember the way, although the snow had made everything look strange. I remembered that there was a tavern called the Crown nearby. I decided not to take a step beyond the tavern, as I'd still another three miles to go to Llwybr Main, and I was so tired that I could barely put one foot in front of the other, and it was still snowing. I was worried that the owners of the Crown had gone to bed, and, believe me, I was heartily pleased to see a light in the kitchen. I was almost too tired to knock on the door, when a young man came to open it, inviting me in. I explained to him my situation, and that I needed a bed there. He went to fetch his mother, and once I had gone over the same story with her, and the two had spoken in private, the mother said:

"I'm sorry, sir, that we can't offer you accommodation, bitter though the night is. We've only the one room not in use, and to tell you the truth that one's haunted, so there wouldn't be any use your trying to sleep in it."

"I'll take my chance with that."

"All right," said the woman, "but I've been honest with you," and off she went to prepare some supper for me, and to tell her daughter to prepare the bed. While I was taking supper, I asked the woman about the ghost, and I got the story from her in full. In brief, it was something like this. They owned the tavern themselves, and had kept the story of the ghost from everyone, so as not to disadvantage the house, for they wanted to sell it quickly. No-one had heard the ghost except for the mother and son, and they hadn't said a word about it to the daughter, whose health was poor, so as not to frighten her, and they charged me not to tell her either, and the mother said:

"The boy and I hear it almost every night, and sometimes more than once during the same night, but, thank the Lord, I don't think the girl's heard anything from it, but she sleeps in the back garret."

"What do you hear?" I asked.

"Well," she said quietly, looking towards the door in case the girl heard, "we hear someone opening the door—there's no lock on it—and then closing it straight away. My husband died in that room about a year ago, and the girl spent so much time tending to him that she lost her health, and I fear in my heart that she might hear the ghost, for it would be the end of her, and I wouldn't mind leaving this place tomorrow if I got a half-decent price for the house."

In a minute the girl came in, and placed a candle on the table for me, and said that my bed was ready, and she bid goodnight. She had a withered and blank look, and I could easily believe that she wasn't well. We all went to our beds. The three rooms where I, the son, and the mother slept were on the same landing, and the girl slept somewhere at the top of the house. Because of my tiredness and the ghost story, I couldn't sleep at all. I had put my revolver on a small table by my side. After a few hours, I thought I heard some noise outside the room. I lit the candle immediately, and grabbed the revolver, for I was determined that if it was some scoundrel who was troubling these innocent people, I would put some holes in him. But when, the next minute, the door opened, I began to tremble like a leaf, and more so when I saw a young girl in her nightclothes heading straight for my bed. Looking tenderly into my eyes, she said quietly:

"Are you better, father dear?" Then she turned on her heel, she closed the door behind her, and I didn't see her afterwards till morning. It was the daughter of the house, poor thing, walking in her sleep. Her anxiety and care for her father during his illness had affected her nerves, and since the day he was buried she had been walking in her sleep every night for a whole year, without her knowing it or her mother and brother. Thus, I was the means of exorcising the ghost of the Crown, and the mother and brother's thanks to me were endless. We became friends forever, and on my travels I'd go to the Crown just as if I was going home, said my Uncle Edward.

15

TUBAL CAIN ADAMS

Of every kind of cruelty, said my Uncle Edward, I think that cruelty to dumb animals is the worst; for the reason that those animals, poor things, cannot testify against their tormentors, and because they are less able to defend themselves and take care of themselves. When I was a boy, I saw many cruel boys, but none like Tubal Cain Adams. He and all his family are dead by now, otherwise I wouldn't tell you this story. And after you've heard it perhaps you'll say that it's very much like an old witch's tale, and smells strongly of the superstitions of the age gone by. But it's a true story, and you may say about it what you like.

Tubal Cain Adams's father was a horse-breaker, and he too was not one of the gentlest ones. I saw a few horses tremble when they heard his voice, and look at his whip with their eyes full of terror. We, the young lads, never liked Tubal to come and play with us, because he would nearly always make sure he'd hurt some of us. After he'd injured one of us, he would always say it had been an accident; but we knew well that he took pleasure from inflicting pain on people. As a result, Tubal was not liked by anybody, and our parents, especially our mothers, would daily have some complaint against him. It was Tubal who taught us to hunt birds. I'm heartily pleased that such vile play has been stamped upon. The way we'd do it was for each of us to take a stick, and go each side of the hedgerow, beating it until we raised a bird, and then we chased the little creature from one end of the hedgerow to the other, unless it flew across the field. The wren would often utterly defeat us, it would disappear as if the earth had swallowed it, and perhaps, after we'd gone a distance from it, we'd hear it twittering cheerfully. The robin would rarely leave the hedgerow, but would fly from branch to branch, back and forth, until it exhausted us, or until it exhausted itself. I'll always remember the last time I went hunting birds with Tubal Cain Adams. It was on a freezing Christmas morning. We'd raised a robin, and had chased him back and forth for a long time, when he alighted on a branch exhausted. And I can imagine this very minute seeing its beautiful little red breast rising and falling rapidly, so quickly was its heart beating. Tubal grabbed it, and that moment broke one of the innocent creature's blood vessels, and blood flowed through its little beak, then it closed its bright eyes, it bowed its head, and died in Tubal's palm. Such a pang of guilt came over me that I couldn't but cry. Seeing me cry, Tubal boxed me on my ear, threw the robin into the air, and hit it with his stick when it was coming down, till its feathers showered all over the place. The occasion affected me greatly, and when I told my mother the story she made me get down on my knees to ask God's forgiveness for the cruelty, something I was more than willing to do. But the feeling of guilt remained with me for a long time, and even now, in my old age, I'm not completely free of it. I could tell you about many of Tubal Cain Adams's cruelties, but I'll tell you, in addition to the one I've already told, only one more.

Years after the robin story, I winced to hear, and that from the parish vicar, that Tubal had taken the nest of a song thrush in which were three chicks. He had taken the nest and the chicks home, and went straight to Robert Lewis, the tailor, and said that his mother wished to borrow a small pair of scissors, scissors for cutting buttonholes. Having got the scissors, and when the chicks were opening their beaks for food, Tubal cut off their tongues. The vicar got to hear of this terrible cruelty, and he went to him and gave him the best lesson he had in his life, and told him that God would certainly make him pay for such an atrocious act. That frightened Tubal quite a bit, and he was a better boy from then on. That's how things were. When Tubal was about eighteen years old, on a Christmas morning, I heard that he was very ill. I went to visit him, and found him almost too feeble to speak. He had broken a blood vessel and had lost a lot of blood. He said: "Edward, do you remember the robin, those years ago?" "Yes, very well," I said. "This is my punishment, isn't it?" he said, and broke down to cry. Tubal recovered from the illness within many months, but he was never strong again. When he was twenty-six years old, he got married. At that time he was working as a farm hand. Within about a year a daughter was born to him, and within five years he had three daughters. But the strange thing was—and here's the moral of the story—all three girls were mutes, and not one of them ever uttered a word. And what was stranger still, all three could hear perfectly well, for deafness nearly always precedes muteness. The mother died giving birth to the last of the daughters, and his children's pitiful condition affected Tubal Cain Adams so much that he soon withered. The girls were taken to the poorhouse, and there one by one they too died. That's the story for you; and do with it as you like, said my Uncle Edward.

16

MY OWN DEAR MOTHER

I had on one occasion disobeyed my mother, and this came to the ears of my Uncle Edward. He didn't let on that he'd heard anything about me, but when I went to his house to listen to him telling his tales, he said:

I am old by now, and although I know that I shan't be here for long, and that the great transformation will have taken place soon enough, I'm not sure that I'm truly like Jesus Christ in any way except in my respect for my mother. One of the finest touches in the Saviour's history is his care for his mother, and that whilst the burden of a world of sins pressed upon Him. If I knew nothing about Him except that one fact, I'd have a high opinion of Him forever. If I had to judge a boy's character by asking him one question only, that question would be—what regard do you have for your mother? Bob, the tumbler, long ago, was considered to be a half-wit, but besides lifting a pin from the floor with his eyelashes, and other feats, Bob said the occasional wise word. Bob said one day: "If you lose your father, you'll have a great loss, but if you lose your mother, you'll lose everything." Even when a boy's character has deteriorated, if I find that he had a high regard for his mother, I have hope of him.

Do you know Dafydd Ddu Eryri's song '*My own dear mother*[1]'? You don't? Well, I'm afraid that many of the boys of this age don't know about the best things in their mother tongue.

[1] Dafydd Ddu Eryri; '*Dafydd the Black of Snowdonia*'; the bardic name of David Thomas (1759–1822), a Welsh-language poet. The song of his that Uncle Edward mentions here, and appears at the end of this story, was not his own original creation (as Owen seems to think) but a translation he made of an English song called '*My Mother*' by Ann Taylor (1782–1866), which is presented here just as Dafydd Ddu's version appears in Owen's story.

I sang that song many times in bygone days, and I don't ever remember singing it without my eyes filling with tears, and I'd sing it for you now if I hadn't lost my voice. There are some old songs, I believe, like verses from Scripture, that have kept many a boy from wrongdoing. I don't know where I'd be today if it weren't for Dafydd Ddu Eryri's song.

When I was young, Wil Williams caused me a lot of harm, as I did him, doubtless. We had a part in every trouble and mischief, although both of us had been taught better things. Wil set his sights on becoming a soldier, and he tried his best to persuade me too to enlist, and I was somewhat inclined towards that. My father had a quick and ill-tempered manner, and I, perhaps, was not the most diligent with my work, and he said one day, in quite a temper, that I was not worth my salt. The comment hurt me greatly, and I answered: "Perhaps not, but I'm going to enlist." "Serves you right, you'll be acceptable for shooting at," said my father, and that hurt me even more.

I went to Wil that evening, and I told him that I'd go with him to Chester to enlist. Wil was glad to hear that, and we decided to set off next morning. After my father had gone to bed, I told my mother about my intention. She wouldn't believe me until I swore that was my intention. She pleaded with me as best she could to change my mind. But I was determined to be a soldier. I got up early the next day, but my mother was up before me, and weeping terribly she pleaded with me again and again not to go away. I had hardened, and thought that I had lost all respect for my parents, and my mother's tears had no effect on me. I can see her this minute watching me set off to meet Wil Williams. I knew little of the pain I was causing her. Having gone almost beyond sight of the house, I looked back. My mother was still at the door, and was drying her eyes with her apron. I began to consider what I was going to do, and that I was, perhaps, taking the very last look at my old home, and something came into my throat, but on I went.

It was a remarkably lovely morning. I remember that that morning was the first time I noticed how beautiful the old neighbourhood was, and I was surprised that I had spent so many years without seeing the splendour of nature. I believe that's the morning I was re-born by nature. Such a thing happens, you know, when a boy discovers for the first time how beautiful this world is. The birds sang pleasantly in the forest nearby, and I thought that the cows, the sheep, and the horses were all looking at me for the last time. I had not, before then, noticed how beautiful these innocent animals were. The narrow stream that ran along the bottom of the long meadow looked clearer than ever, and when I saw a rat running from my path as I went past I didn't have the slightest inclination to kill it. When I went through the gate of the furthest field, I left it open, for I had this notion, that if I closed it I'd never return, and I began to think about far-off countries, and about fighting the Blacks, about hardship, cold, and hunger. But my father had said that I wasn't worth my salt, and I went on resolutely.

I had to go past Hafod Lom, and I thought about Doli'r Hafod. I was very fond of Doli even then, but I've already told you that story. Before reaching Yr Hafod there was a narrow, low, watery road, with a high hedge on both sides of it, and as I was walking along this road I could hear someone singing. It was Doli, singing whilst milking. Having drawn near, I sat on the bank to listen to her. If she had known that I was on the other side of the hedge, she wouldn't have sang, I know. Doli had a most enchanting voice, in my opinion, and I'd never heard it so enchanting as it was that morning. I sat to listen to her for the last time in my life, as I thought, and the first words I heard were the fifth verse of the song 'My own dear mother'. Something deep in my heart awoke, and I returned home, and I think that my respect for my mother from that day forth increased and increased throughout the rest of her life.

Wil Williams took great offence because I hadn't gone to meet him, called me a coward, and went straight to Chester to enlist.

Afterwards, he was sent to India, and nobody heard the slightest mention of him again.

Perhaps you would like to hear the words to the song, '*My own Dear Mother*'?

> Who fed me from her gentle breast,
> And hush'd me in her arms to rest,
> And on my cheek sweet kisses prest?
> > *My Mother.*
>
> When sleep forsook my open eye,
> Who was it sung sweet hushaby,
> And rock'd me that I should not cry?
> > *My Mother.*
>
> Who sat and watch'd my infant head,
> When sleeping on my cradle bed,
> And tears of sweet affection shed?
> > *My Mother.*
>
> When pain and sickness made me cry,
> Who gaz'd upon my heavy eye,
> And wept, for fear that I should die?
> > *My Mother.*
>
> Who drest my doll in clothes so gay,
> And taught me pretty how to play,
> And minded all I had to say?
> > *My Mother.*
>
> Who ran to help me when I fell,
> And would some pretty story tell,
> Or kiss the place to make it well?
> > *My Mother.*

Who taught my infant lips to pray,
And love God's holy book and day,
And walk in wisdom's pleasant way?
    My Mother.

And can I ever cease to be
Affectionate and kind to thee,
Who wast so very kind to me,
    My Mother.

Ah! no, the thought I cannot bear;
And if God please my life to spare,
I hope I shall reward thy care,
    My Mother.

When thou art feeble, old, and gray,
My healthy arm shall be thy stay,
And I will soothe thy pains away,
    My Mother.

And when I see thee hang thy head,
'Twill be my turn to watch thy bed,
And tears of sweet affection shed,
    My Mother.

For God, who lives above the skies,
Would look with vengeance in His eyes,
If I should ever dare despise,
    My Mother.

17

AN OLD CHARACTER

So Ned Sibion's dead, is he? said my Uncle Edward. One of the strangest creatures I saw in my life, and one of the most difficult things under the sun would be to describe his character precisely. Ned had to be seen, heard, and known before an idea could be formed about the delight of his character, and the world is poorer for his loss. I've no idea why, but strange old characters are getting rarer each day. As Wil Bryan[1] said years ago, education or something makes us all the same as postage stamps.

Ned Sibion was a nickname; the man's name was Edward Williams, and I think he hailed from the parish of Ysgeifiog. The family had a knack of nurturing nicknames, and his father was called 'Old Grothe'—I remember him well. Poor Ned was a few inches short of a yard, which was probably why I never heard that anyone hated him. Ned had married three times, and the three wives were very similar to one another, and to him. There's a rook for every rook. All three had had to submit to the same rule—namely, to live with him for a month's trial before he married them, so that he could judge their temper. Ned was one of the least lazy men I ever saw, and, whether he was collecting rags or something else, he'd always do so at a furious pace, as busy as a busybody. Although he was very honest, he would never look anyone in the eye, and if he stopped to talk to someone, his eyes would be scouting around his feet. It was as if he had been intended by Providence to find things, and indeed, people said that he had found much during his life.

---

[1] Wil Bryan is a central character in Owen's novel *Rhys Lewis*, and a minor character in another, *Enoc Huws*. A likeable rouge whose intelligence is expressed by wit rather than sophistication, he is one of Owen's most enduring creations, and clearly one of his own favourites.

Ned would get up with the dawn after every fair and market, and his eyes would be combing every street for something he could find. Every Sunday morning during the summer months Ned would have eyed every nook and cranny of every street before other people had risen from their beds, and, to salve his conscience probably, would sing a hymn on the Sabbath morn. I heard him tens of times from my bed. Whatever the words, he always sang the same tune, a tune, I think, of his own composition—some kind of minor-key chant—particularly Welsh in sound. Ned would not continue to search like this throughout his life had he not occasionally found things. I remember once that a man got so drunk on a Saturday evening that he lost his watch, and had no earthly idea where. But he got the watch from Ned on Sunday afternoon, and didn't give the honest creature a penny of a reward. This, I suspect, taught Ned to keep everything he found from then on.

Ned had very little idea of distance. One harvest time, Professor Edwards was walking down Foregate Street in Chester, and who did he see, with a sickle under his arm, but Ned. He went up to him, and said to him:

"Well, Edward, what are you doing here?"

"I'm going down to London, Mr Edwards, to the harvest—they say London's a great place at harvest-time," said Ned.

That's how it was. Within a week the Professor was coming down the street in Mold, and who did he see but Ned, and he said:

"Hello, Edward, I thought you were going to London to the harvest?"

"Well, no, Mr Edwards," said Ned, "I got no closer to London than Parkgate (Parkgate in Cheshire), you see."

I'll warrant that there are two hundred yards between Ned's house and the well where he got water; and one day I saw him going to the well with two huge pitchers. Having filled them with water, he carried one a short distance and put it down, then he fetched the other and placed it beside the first. And that's how he carried them till he came to the house. I asked why he did thus. "To save time, you see," said Ned.

Ned didn't have much of an idea about the value of money, either. Once, after dark, Ned went to Thomas Roberts, Tŷ Draw[2], to buy a hen, and after Mr Roberts had caught the hen under the open shed, they began haggling about the price.

"How much do you want for it, Mr Roberts?" said Ned.

"Well," said Mr Roberts, "you can have it for fifteen."

"Well, no, I wont, I'll give you eighteen, if you like," said Ned.

"But I'm saying you can have it for fifteen," said Mr Roberts.

"I'll give you eighteen, and not a farthing more," said Ned.

"All right," said Mr Roberts, and gave him three pence back.

Once, Ned was labouring for Mr Joseph Eaton for two shillings and four pence a day; but he was missed Monday and Tuesday. When he arrived at his work on Wednesday morning, Mr Eaton said to him:

"Well, Edward, where were you yesterday and the day before?"

"I went to Flint to gather cockles, Mr Eaton," said Ned.

"Did you do well?" asked his master.

" Yes," said Ned, "very well indeed. I gathered an unconscionable load of them, and I took them to Rhuthun yesterday, and got twenty pence for them."

"Well, as well as walking for thirty miles, you've lost three shillings in wages," said Mr Eaton.

"Say what you like, I did splendidly," said Ned.

Sometimes Ned would change his mind very suddenly. I remember on one occasion I wanted to move the dung heap, and I knew that Ned did jobs of that sort, and when I saw him I asked him to come and do the work. "I'll come and have a look at it," said Ned; and that afternoon I saw him sizing up the dung heap. Although your aunt knew Ned well, she'd never heard him speak, and she said she'd come with me to the yard to listen to us making

---

[2] '*Tŷ Draw*' translates either as '*The House Beyond*' or '*The House Yonder*'.

a bargain. I charged her not to laugh, or she'd be certain to spoil the bargain, for Ned couldn't bear being laughed at. She promised to be quite discreet, and into the yard we went. After Ned had spent a great deal of time sizing up the dung heap, we at last agreed that I would pay him half a crown to move it, and your aunt could barely keep herself from laughing as she heard Ned speak so childishly.

"But you remember, Edward," I said, "you must move it early on Monday morning."

"Well," said Ned, "if it's fine ("*teehee*—" said your aunt) I won't come," and off he went, and he didn't come to move the dung heap. Your aunt by laughing had spoiled everything, and made Ned change his mind in the middle of the sentence.

For a time, Ned lived in one of the cabins below the entry at the top of Henffordd, and then his main business was collecting old rags. By some chance he had found a pair of small wheels on axles. He spent some days making the wagon, and after he finished he set off with it to collect rags, but the wagon was wider than the entry, and he couldn't get it through, and seeing him in trouble, his neighbour Drury said to him:

"Well, Edward, your wagon's too wide."

"No, it's not," said Ned, "it's the entry that's too narrow," and he went into the house in a foul temper, and fetched a hammer and smashed the wagon, the wheels and the whole lot into splinters.

I don't know how things are with Ned by now; but I find it pretty hard to believe that the Lord Almighty will be hard on him—he was so harmless. The religious tendency was not strong in Ned; and yet he couldn't leave religion alone. He rarely attended Sabbath services, but it was even more rare for him to be absent from any preaching festival, no matter which denomination held the festival. In an Association meeting, or a convention or a preaching festival, Ned would be very prominent. But I'd worry that the reason he came to these meetings was in order to show off his buttons, as on such occasions the large and bright buttons on his coat and waistcoat drew everyone's attention. And yet it's not my place to judge Ned's motivations. Perhaps Ned considered that the best way for him to glorify God was through his buttons. And who can say?

Although Ned, no more than a gatepost, didn't know the difference between a Liberal and a Tory, he boasted that he was a Liberal to his core, and when the act giving the vote to all householders was passed, and he understood that he had a vote, no one could deal with him. I remember as if it was yesterday the first election after the act became law. Ned was up and dressed in his best before seven o'clock in the morning, his buttons shining. He told everyone he met that he had no intention of voting for one side or the other. Understanding this, he was harassed by the most influential Tories for hours on end, and Ned ran away from them like a hare, over the roads and the fields, until he made everybody tired. But about quarter of an hour before the poll closed, Ned came near the place of his own accord, and rested his back against the wall as if to challenge everybody. The most prominent people of the two parties implored him to vote; but Ned replied: "If the Apostle Paul himself asked me to vote, I wouldn't." In a minute the Liberal Agent came past—a wiser man than most—and, seeing the big crowd around Ned trying to persuade him to vote, he said:

"What's wrong with you, people? Do you think that Edward doesn't know how and for whom to vote, without your teaching him? Leave the man alone. Edward knows that there are only five minutes before the poll closes," and went away. Ned went straight to the poll and voted for the Liberals. After he came out, Ned was dressed with yellow ribbons, and was carried on the Liberals' shoulders up and down the town for hours, and in my life I never saw so much merriment and innocent fun at an election, and Ned Sibion rejoiced in the honour bestowed upon him. Well, well, and poor Ned is dead! Do you know what? I shall miss him terribly, said my Uncle Edward.

18

TOO ALIKE

Have you ever wondered, said my Uncle Edward, that although there are so many people in the world, and that everybody's face is of the same form and design, how rarely you find two faces that are so similar to each other that you can't rightly tell, when looking at them, that there's much difference between them? This is a real blessing; and I see as much of the Creator's wisdom in this as in anything. One of the things I hate most in the world is to see some who are so similar to each other, like twins, and there's a good reason why. Here's a curious story from my own life—almost too curious to be believed, but you can believe it or not.

When I was about twenty-eight years old, I had some business to go to Oswestry. It would take too much time to tell you what the business was, but, in brief, I wanted to see a man about an important matter, and he had promised to meet me in Oswestry at the horse fair. Because of the distance, and lest I missed him, I had made a point of arriving in the town the evening before the fair. I got pretty comfortable lodgings in a private house. I'd known very well for years that some of my mother's family lived near Oswestry, but because of some quarrel, there had been no connection between us and them. As far as I could remember, I'd never seen any of them, and I had no intention of visiting them, or of enquiring after them. "Don't have anything to do with them; if they can do without us, we can do without them," said my mother when I was setting off, and I thought no more about them.

I had never been to Oswestry before, and the morning after I wandered a fair bit to see the town, for the horse fair didn't start until mid-day. Turning a street corner, I came face-to-face with an enormous policeman, and he stared at me as if I had horns on my head. I couldn't understand why the man was staring at me like that, for there was nothing peculiar about my clothes, for nearly all farmers in those days wore homespun cloth. I thought that there was nothing in particular in me that might draw attention except my hair—which, when I was young, was crow-black, and curly like a little lamb's wool. I must confess to you my weakness, I thought rather a lot of my hair, for I had never seen its like. That was it, and I thought no more about the policeman. I wandered another hour about the town until I was tired, and I turned into a tavern to rest awhile. Nobody thought anything of such a thing in those days. I'll warrant that I'd been in the tavern for a quarter of an hour in a room by myself whiling away the time, when a man about the same age as I came in, and so similar in appearance to me that it frightened me to look at him. His hair was black and curly like mine, and his face exactly like mine, and there wasn't a great difference in the colour of his clothes. Were it not for the fact that I knew it was impossible, I would have sworn that I myself was the man. I could see that he too had been struck by the similarity, but he didn't say a word. He walked up and down the room for a bit, then stood and gazed through the window into the road; and without calling for anything to drink, he slipped out quietly through a door that looked to me like the back door of the house. Within two minutes, the policeman that I'd seen earlier entered the room, and said:

"Well, John Jones, you've come home at last?"

"My name is Edward Jones, and it seems you've mistaken me for the man who's just gone out," I said.

"A story like that won't work on me, John, I know you far too well, and you'd better come with me straight away."

Not having been away from home much I was quite innocent, and was very frightened. I protested that I wasn't John Jones, whoever he was; and I told, short-winded, a little of my history, and gave my oath that I'd never in my life been in Oswestry before now. But nothing I said to the policeman had any more effect on him other than to make him smile mockingly, and he said:

"John, you might as well put a stop to this right now; making up lies will do you no earthly good. Come with me quietly and calmly."

"What's the accusation against me?" I asked.

"A parson doesn't need to hear the Lord's Prayer," he said.

I called the landlady, expecting some help from her, but she only made my situation worse. She swore on her strong point that no other man had been in the tavern whilst I was there, and she called the maid and she swore the same thing.

"Can't you see, John, that lying won't do you any earthly good?" said the policeman.

"Wait a moment," said the landlady, "Isn't he John Jones of Tan'rallt[1]? Well, how comical of me that I shouldn't recognise the man?"

"Likely you were comical," said the policeman.

"You're surely making a mistake," I said, and I nearly cried.

"I saw Mary yesterday, and she was telling me about you, John," the maid told me quietly, and I could have hit her.

"Here you are, John," said the policeman, "if you don't come with me quietly and calmly, I'll have to handcuff you, but I've no wish to make a show of you."

"Yes, go, my lad, without making a fuss," said the landlady.

And go I did—indeed, I had no choice—I had to go, but I expected that they would learn of their mistake. It was a market day, as I said, and hundreds of eyes were looking at me as I was escorted by the policeman through the town, and a crowd of children would have followed us had the policeman not threatened them. I felt my face burning like fire, and could hear this person and the other saying:

"What's this one done, I wonder?"

---

[1] '*Tan'rallt*' translates as '*Underhill*'.

"Nothing good, you can be sure."

"Such a pity, he looks respectable."

"Those are often the worst."

One or two of those I passed gave me the credit that I obviously felt my situation, and so I did, sure enough. I looked from beneath my frown to see if I could find anyone in the fair who knew me, but to no avail, and perhaps that's what caused one, who looked like a shepherd, to remark as I passed him:

"He's a sheep-killing dog, you can be sure."

Well, I was taken to the roundhouse, and there was no earthly point in my protesting, explaining myself, asking for an explanation, or anything else; the only answer I got was that I could tell everything to the magistrate the next morning. That was a horrid afternoon; I shall remember it always, and I didn't sleep a wink on my wooden bed that night, and sometimes I thought the whole thing was a dream. To cut a long story short, I was brought before my betters— the only time in my life. There was only one magistrate on the bench, thinking no doubt that it would be a case of remand, and I thought from his appearance that I'd get fair play from him, and perhaps some redress for my having been wrongly imprisoned. He said:

"Well, John Jones, what was it that made you leave your wife and children?"

"My name isn't John Jones, sir, and I never had any wife, let alone children," I said, and I began to say who I was and where I was from, but I was stopped immediately by the magistrate. And he said:

"John, John, you've become hardened in wickedness—we know you all too well," and he called for Mary Jones, and a poor-looking woman came forward, and the magistrate said:

"Mary Jones, is this man your husband?"

"Yes, sir," said the woman, "but he's terribly altered, and I'm very glad to see him. He was never cruel to me, and I don't know what made him leave me and the children four years ago. I hope, Mr Price, you won't be harsh on him, for I'm sure he'll come home to his family now, won't you, John *bach*?" And the woman broke down to cry.

By now I was certain that I'd been bewitched, or had fallen down Elian's well[2]. The magistrate said:

"Well, John, I should put you in jail for three months—that's what you should get for abandoning your family. But the parish has kept them long enough, and if you promise to go home, and look after your wife and children, you may go free this once. If you do not promise to do so, I shall have to give you three months. What do you say, John?"

I thought that minute that I could escape after I'd been freed, and I said:

"Well, I shall try my best to do as you ask, sir."

"Very good," said the magistrate, "but make sure you don't come before me again, for it won't be like this for you next time. It's a terrible shame that a good craftsman like you, John—one who's a father of children, and coming from a respectable family—has made himself a subject of talk. May this be a lesson for you forever, John. You may go now."

I was bewildered. The woman came up to me to shake my hand, and I gave my hand to her, limply enough. She had been crying—of happiness, I suppose—till she was half-blind. While I was walking by her side, without knowing where I was going or what to do, the woman looked at me every fifteen seconds or so, as if doubting her eyes, and she spoke of a hundred things of which I knew nothing. She said more than once that I was terribly altered, but that she was pleased so see me so tidy. She spoke of the children, and told me that it wasn't all her fault when I went away, and she looked intently at my face again and again. I didn't say a word to her any

---

[2] Saint Elian's well, near Colwyn Bay, was one of many so-called 'Cursing Wells' in Wales, where people came to ask for their enemies to be cursed. Early in the nineteenth century, its owner is recorded to have made as much as £300 a year by charging people to curse others at the well, or to have their curses lifted. The well has now been filled in.

more than a mute, and I was afraid I was losing my senses. She led me to some yard where there were a number of houses, and all the neighbours were standing in the doorways, smiling at me and congratulating me. It was clear that I was welcomed back. All the way the woman burst into tears every two minutes, and I felt truly sorry for her. The two boys were playing with other children in the yard, and as we went into the house, Mary Jones called them to come and see their father. The children came in, but I took no notice of them—I couldn't stand seeing them, the poor things. This made Mary cry again, and she said:

"Why don't you say something to the children, John, if you refuse to speak to me."

Mercifully, the children wouldn't come near me. I noticed that the house, although poor, was very clean; and after she finished crying, Mary said:

"You can imagine, John, that I am poor; do you have some money for me to get you something to eat?"

I gave her a few shillings, and after she put the kettle on the fire she set off, and before long returned with her apron full of things from the shop. Right behind her the man I'd seen in the tavern came in. He hugged and kissed the children, and his wife likewise. Mary looked as if she were deranged. I cannot describe the scene for you or my happiness. The man had returned to his family, but when he saw the policeman coming after him into the tavern he fled. Having understood that I'd been mistaken for him, but that the Bench had forgiven me on the condition that I looked after my family, John came straight home. He was full of regret that he had left his wife and children. We had tea together comfortably enough, and after some discussion I learned that he was my cousin Jac. I came home faster than as fast as I could, and along the way I looked at everyone in case I saw someone else who looked like me. When I told my mother the story, she said:

"Yes, that's them, for sure, no luck follows them."

19

THE TWO FAMILIES

I fear, said my Uncle Edward, that there's a tendency for some people these days to think that God has nothing to do with man's temporal circumstances. Indeed, I've heard some say boldly enough that it's all luck and chance and every-man-for-himself in this life. And in a sense it's no wonder that some people believe that, for we see how often the evil, dishonest man succeeds, and the good and sincere man fails. But among those who were considered good people that failed with whom I came into contact during my life, I could, almost without exception, put my finger on the reason for their failure. Some cancer, that wasn't visible to everyone, was the cause of it all. If you will live long enough, and take careful notice of families and things, you'll soon find that Providence brings things to order, and that it corrects itself in the end—rewarding goodness and punishing evil. Here's a story for you about two families that I knew well, and it's as true as anything that was ever said. But wait a minute. I hear you've been printing some of the stories I'm telling you, and because some members of those two families are still alive, I'll give them different names.

In Dyffryn Maelor, many years ago, there was a young farmer who had just got married and who rented one of the best farms in the country. I'll call him Mr Jones, Y Wern[1]. I don't know now, even if I ever knew, how he managed to take such a good farm; but I do know that he was totally uneducated. He was a hard-working and skilful man, and his wife was as skilful as he, and the world was with them and their success was obvious to everyone. Whilst Mr and Mrs Jones allowed no-one to beat them in the fair and in

---

[1] 'Y Wern' translates as 'Damp Meadow' or as 'Alder-grove'.

the market or in cultivating the farm and in animal husbandry, they were second to none in their attendance and generosity at the chapel. The neighbours well knew that the Wern family, besides increasing their stock daily, were also putting money away, and their reputation was high in their landlord's mind. Years passed and many children were born to them. Mr Jones had been made to feel the disadvantage of being uneducated many times, and he made sure that he gave his children the best education available in the area, and after they reached the requisite age, he apprenticed some of the boys to shopkeepers. Mr Jones by now had became quite a wealthy man, when, one day, a good-looking and well-schooled young sawyer came to the neighbourhood. I'll call him Mr Bellis. Bellis was no more than a common craftsman working for eighteen shillings a week, but he was a skilled and crafty man. As he was a member of the same chapel as Mr Jones, Bellis and the Wern family soon became good friends. Eventually, Bellis persuaded Mr Jones to invest in the timber trade—that he, Bellis, had the knowledge, and Mr Jones the money, and he drew a pleasant picture of the great profit that could be made in the business. The two became partners—the one with knowledge the other with money. This continued for years. Without going into detail, the result was that Mr Jones became poorer and poorer each day, and Bellis became richer. In the partnership, the stoutest part of the stick was in the knowledge's hand, that is, Bellis's. In the end the partnership was terminated, and Mr Jones found himself worse off by several hundred pounds than was the case when the wife was his only partner. The boys were forced out into the world to earn their living, and I could tell you about the hard effort they had of it; but God was with the boys. By now Bellis too had got married, and the first thing he did after breaking off his connection with Mr Jones was to buy a large mill, and he soon became a famous merchant, and not only that, but an a illustrious man in the denomination to which he belonged. He collected heaps of money and raised his children to hold respectable positions.

But both Jones and Bellis died, and there was a pleasant aroma the day one of them was buried, and quite a show the day the other was buried. But where are their offspring now? Although Bellis's children were once rolling in money, they and their riches have gone from the earth, and some of them lie in the drunkard's grave. But as for the lineage of the Wern family—offspring and issue—Providence dripped fat on their paths and everything they did prospered. The names of those amongst them who are at rest from their labours are held dearly by those that knew them, and many of them are still alive, useful, and one or two of them fill the highest offices and receive the highest honours the country can bestow upon them. As you proceed in life, notice how Providence always levels things, said my Uncle Edward.

ALSO IN THE DANIEL OWEN
SIGNATURE SERIES

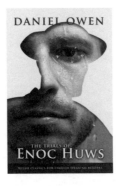

The Trials of Enoc Huws by Daniel Owen.
ISBN 978-0-9567031-0-1

This enthralling tale of love, hypocrisy and misunderstanding is set against the backdrop of a small town in Victorian North Wales. The local lead mine is being worked by its unscrupulous owner, Captain Trefor, with no hope of any returns for the unfortunate investors who have entrusted their wealth to the Captain. When love blossoms between the Captain's self-confident daughter, Susi, and the naïve and upright Enoc Huws, dramatic complications ensue.

A classic novel by Daniel Owen, the foremost Welsh-language novelist of the 19th century, *Profedigaethau Enoc Huws* was first published in 1891. With its astute observations of human nature and local characters, the novel has enjoyed immense popularity with Welsh readers for over 100 years. One of the acknowledged masterpieces of the Welsh language, it has been adapted for stage and television (in an early 1974 TV adaptation, and later as *Y Dreflan* on S4C).

Profedigaethau Enoc Huws was translated into English from its original Welsh by Claud Vivian and serialised in the newspaper Wales. It has never before been published as a book in English. This revised and updated translation by the international poet, comedian and writer, Les Barker, reinstates for the modern reader the wit and colloquial colour of the novel's original Welsh.

Number of pages 384